DEEP TROUBLE II

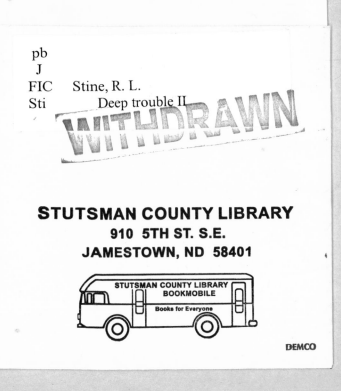

ALL-NEW! ALL-TERRIFYING!

#1 Revenge of the Living Dummy
Also Available on Audiobook from Scholastic Audiobooks

#2 Creep from the Deep
Also Available on Audiobook from Scholastic Audiobooks

#3 Monster Blood for Breakfast

#4 The Scream of the Haunted Mask

#5 Dr. Maniac vs. Robby Schwartz

NOW WITH BONUS FEATURES!
LOOK IN THE BACK OF THE BOOK FOR EXCLUSIVE AUTHOR INTERVIEWS AND MORE.

Night of the Living Dummy

Deep Trouble

Monster Blood

The Haunted Mask

One Day at HorrorLand
(INCLUDES A SECRET GUIDE TO HORRORLAND!)

Goosebumps®

DEEP TROUBLE II

R. L. STINE

SCHOLASTIC INC.
New York Toronto London Auckland Sydney
Mexico City New Delhi Hong Kong Buenos Aires

ISBN 0-439-83780-4

12 11 10 9 8 7 6 5   8 9 10 11/0

Printed in the U.S.A.   .   40

DEEP TROUBLE II

I'm back.

That's what I thought when I arrived on the *Cassandra* for another summer vacation.

Yes, I, William Deep, Jr., world-famous undersea explorer, am back.

One year older. One year wiser. One year tougher.

I breathed in a big gulp of salty air. I gazed at the clear green Caribbean sea around me.

My little sister, Sheena, stood beside me. But I pretended she wasn't there.

She sort of ruined the atmosphere for me. She usually does.

The *Cassandra* is my uncle's boat. It's a floating research lab.

My uncle, Dr. George Deep, is a marine biologist. My parents sent me and Sheena to visit him on our summer vacation. They sent us the year before too.

Dr. D. lives on the boat in the Caribbean all year long, studying tropical fish. It's fun for us. We get to swim and stuff. My uncle is really nice. And my parents figure we'll learn a lot about science and ocean life while we're with him.

Last summer I made one of the most shocking discoveries in the history of marine biology.

I found a mermaid. A real mermaid.

No one believed me, of course. I wasn't a grown-up scientist. I was a twelve-year-old boy on vacation in the Caribbean.

Know-it-all Sheena thought I was lying.

My uncle, Dr. D., thought I was making it up. He didn't believe in mermaids.

Until I proved him wrong.

We didn't tell anyone about the mermaids. Some really bad guys wanted to capture them and put them in cages. To protect the mermaids, Sheena, Dr. D., and I agreed to keep them a secret.

So the world will never know . . .

And now, I'm back! I told myself. *Billy Deep, one of the greatest explorers in the seven seas.*

And I'm not a twelve-year-old kid anymore.

I'm thirteen.

And this summer, I'm going to find something big. Something even more amazing than a mermaid.

This time, the world will hear about it. This time I'll be famous.

I hope.

* * *

The fire coral glowed bright red. I snorkeled near it, careful not to touch it.

I'd stepped on fire coral once before. It burned my foot like crazy.

They don't call it fire coral for nothing.

I studied the coral wall. Neon-bright fish darted in and out of the delicate holes. It was beautiful. There, under the water, everything seemed calm. Quiet. Peaceful.

But I knew better. I was an experienced snorkeler. A snorkeling hero.

An untrained swimmer wouldn't have noticed it. That little ripple in the water. The way the fish all suddenly disappeared.

But I felt it. That whiff of danger.

Something was coming. Something deadly.

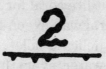

I whirled around — and faced the intruder.

A giant octopus!

"WHOOOA!" The snorkel flew from my mouth as I cried out in shock. An octopus! It rose up in the water, its purple body *as big as mine*!

I shoved the mouthpiece back into my mouth. And frantically tried to thrash away from it.

But before I could get moving, I felt something cold and soft wrap around my throat.

Ohhhh.

A tentacle as thick as a human arm.

Its suction pods snapped to my skin. It started to pull me . . . pull me down.

No!

Gasping for breath, I lifted my head out of the water. And let out a choked cry for help.

I felt another cold tentacle slide around my waist. And then another around my chest.

I thrashed and kicked. But the huge creature was too powerful. The big suction pods made loud

4

sucking sounds as they tightened against my skin.

The tentacles pulled me . . . pulled me . . .

Until everything went black.

No! No!

I wasn't losing consciousness. The blackness that washed around me was octopus ink.

I shut my eyes. Twisted and squirmed.

But the tentacles pulled harder. Pulled me down into the inky blackness.

I choked and sputtered. And struggled up to the surface.

The water tossed and churned, black with octopus ink.

The big suction pods bit into my bare skin.

The tentacles tightened . . . tightened around my ribs, my stomach.

I couldn't breathe. Couldn't move.

I'm going under, I realized. I'm doomed. Doomed!

My lungs felt about to explode.

No! I thought. I can't die! Not like this!

There must be a way to make the octopus let go.

With a last burst of strength, I slid my right arm free.

Now what? *Now what?*

I stretched a finger toward its throbbing, purple belly.

Red and yellow stars flashed before my eyes. I knew I had little time. I was about to pass out any second.

I reached toward the big throbbing body. With my last bit of strength, I wriggled my fingers.

Please let this work, I prayed.

Please . . .

Then I started tickling.

My fingers tickled the purple belly.

Tickle, tickle!

The octopus squirmed.

Tickle, tickle!

The tentacles relaxed.

Yes! Yes! It's working! The octopus was ticklish!

Its big body heaved — and it shoved me away.

"Stop it, Billy!" the octopus whined. "I hate your stupid jokes. Stop tickling me!"

Then the octopus pinched me.

Okay, okay. So it *wasn't* an octopus. It was my little sister, Sheena.

Sheena always spoils my fun. She has no imagination. She hates to pretend.

Well . . . it's true that she doesn't look much like an octopus. She looks a lot like me, actually. Skinny, with straight black hair. Hers is long, and mine is short. We both have dark blue eyes and bushy dark eyebrows.

She's younger than I am. She's only eleven. But she acts like an old lady sometimes. She hates games. She likes cold, hard facts.

"What were you pretending this time?" Sheena teased. "That you were a tickle-fish?"

"None of your business," I answered. She would never admit that I was a great undersea explorer. Had she forgotten about the mermaids?

It didn't matter. Other little sisters look up to their big brothers. Not Sheena.

If I told her I was pretending she was an octopus, she'd never stop teasing me.

"You're a moron, Billy," she groaned.

Do you believe she calls a great undersea explorer a *moron*?

"I'll show you," I replied lamely.

I love to play tricks on Sheena. It isn't easy to fool her.

But I had an idea. I thought of a mean trick to play on her that would scare her — but good.

I swam back to the boat.

I flipped my mask up and climbed aboard the *Cassandra*. It was a big, sturdy boat, about fifty feet long, with a large open deck. Below deck were research labs, a galley, and a few cabins for sleeping.

The white deck steamed in the sun, deserted. It was about noon.

Dr. D. must be down below, I realized. Perfect.

I didn't want him to see me and blow my trick.

8

I reached under a stack of life jackets. I pulled out a square, gray vinyl pillow I'd hidden there.

I stared out toward the reef. Sheena was busy snorkeling. She wasn't looking.

Good.

Here was my plan: I was going to swim underwater, holding the gray pillow over my head. I'd hold it so one of the corners pointed up. You guessed it. Like a shark's fin.

Then I'd swim at Sheena as fast as I could. She'd think a shark was headed straight for her!

It would scare her to death. I couldn't wait to hear her screaming to me for help.

"We'll see who's a moron," I murmured to myself.

I slipped back into the water. Holding the pillow in sharkfin position, I started kicking. I swam underwater toward the reef. Toward Sheena.

After a few minutes, I bobbed up for breath. She hadn't seen me yet.

Holding the "sharkfin" high, I paddled closer. Closer.

Then I heard them. At last. The screams.

"Shark!" Sheena wailed. "Help! A shark!"

Ha! Ha! Excellent screaming, Sheena!

I finally fooled Miss Know-It-All!

"Shaaark!" she wailed again.

I couldn't stay underwater any longer. I had to rise up so I could laugh in her face.

I popped my head above the water.

Hey! Sheena was swimming frantically toward the boat. She was still screaming like crazy.

But she wasn't looking in my direction. She hadn't even seen me.

"Shark!" she cried again. She made a frightened motion toward the reef.

I saw it too. A huge sharkfin! A *real* one!

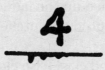

4

"Huh?" I let out a terrified gasp.

The shark was as big as a *whale*!

Where did it come from? Dr. D. had told us there were no large sharks in the area.

I guess no one told the shark!

It rose up, tossed by a wave. And I gaped at its silvery-white body — as long as a canoe!

It snapped its massive jaws. The *CRAACK* echoed over the water.

"Whooooa!" I let go of the pillow and paddled for the boat as fast as I could. My heart raced. The water felt as thick as mud. Why couldn't I swim faster?

"Hurry, Billy!" Sheena called. I glanced back.

The gigantic gray fin cut through the water like a powerboat.

The shark sped straight for us.

"Swim!" I ordered myself. "Faster! Faster!"

Sheena and I thrashed toward the boat. I didn't

glance back again. I didn't want to see how close the big shark was!

Gasping, my entire body aching, I reached the *Cassandra*. I grabbed the side. Almost safe. Almost.

Sheena scrambled up the ladder ahead of me.

"Hurry!" I shouted. I clutched the ladder and glanced back.

The shark roared closer. So close, I could see its glassy black eyes. And its mouth full of jagged teeth.

"Sheena, go!" I screamed. I shoved her up onto the deck and scrambled up the ladder.

"We made it!" Sheena gasped.

Gasping for breath, my chest heaving, I stared over the rail.

The shark kept coming! Like a submarine with teeth!

"NOOOO!"

I let out a hoarse wail as the huge fish slammed into the side of the boat!

"NOOOOOO!"

The whole boat rocked — and tilted.

I grabbed the rail and held on.

"Hold on, Sheena!" I shouted. "It's attacking!"

I braced myself for another jolt.

Nothing happened.

The shark disappeared into the churning water.

Dr. D. appeared on deck, looking confused. "What's going on?" he cried.

Sheena and I ran to him, screaming, "A shark! A shark!"

"What?" Dr. D. stared out to sea.

The water gleamed calmly now. Soft waves splashed against the side of the boat.

The monster shark had vanished.

"Billy — there is nothing out there. What are you talking about?" Dr. D. demanded.

"There *was* a shark! A huge shark! It chased us," Sheena cried breathlessly. "It crashed into the boat!"

"A shark?" Dr. D. shook his head. "No way. No way a shark could make the boat rock like that."

"But it was HUGE!" I screamed. "It was as big as *ten* sharks!"

"As big as *twenty* sharks!" Sheena exclaimed.

Dr. D. rubbed his bald spot. "I told you two before. I checked the radar. I checked out all of my sonic surveyors. There are no large sharks in this area."

He stared me in the eye and asked, "Are you sure, Billy? Are you sure you saw a shark?"

"We're sure!" Sheena insisted. We both knew he'd believe her before he'd believe me.

"Come down to the lab with me, kids," Dr. D. said.

We followed him below deck to one of the labs. Dr. D. pointed to a large tank in the corner. It held a silvery fish the size of a big dog.

Sheena gasped. "Wow! I've never seen a fish like that before!"

"Neither have I," Dr. D. said solemnly. "That's what bothers me."

I stared at the fish as it swam around in the tank. It looked sort of familiar, but I didn't know why.

"I can't identify it," Dr. D. went on. "I've never seen a fish this size that looks like this. I've been searching through all my books, but I can't find it!"

He pointed to a stack of books on marine biology. I picked one up and flipped through it. It had page after page of cool color photos of all kinds of fish.

Dr. D. glanced over my shoulder as I examined the book. "It can't be in that section, Billy," he told me. "All those fish are tiny."

I turned a page, looking for the big fish section. Then I turned another page — and gasped.

Dr. D. gripped my shoulder as he stared down at the photo with me. "No!" he cried. "It can't be!"

5

We crowded around the book, staring at the photo. It showed a fish exactly like the one in the tank. Thin, silvery . . . but there was one huge difference.

"It's a minnow!" Dr. D. exclaimed. "But that's impossible!"

I read the words under the picture. "'Tropical minnow, one inch long.'"

I glanced at the fish in the tank. It was more like four feet long!

Dr. D.'s eyes narrowed as he studied the fish. "How could a minnow get so huge?" he wondered out loud. "I must examine it more closely."

Sheena and I stood behind him, watching. He studied the picture of the minnow through a magnifying glass. Then he turned to the giant minnow, staring at its scales, checking every mark.

"The markings are exactly the same," Dr. D. murmured.

"Can I look through the magnifying glass?" Sheena asked.

"Sure." Dr. D. passed the glass to her.

"A minnow . . . ," Dr. D. murmured. "How can this giant fish be a minnow? It's supposed to be as small as your goldfish, Billy."

My goldfish! "Whoops," I cried. "I forgot to feed my goldfish this morning."

"Better go do it," Dr. D. said.

I started toward the lab door. On my way, I spotted a cabinet filled with glass bottles. "What's in these, Dr. D.?" I asked.

He turned away from the monster minnow to look. "Oh, that's plankton," he replied. "It's made of tiny little plants and animals that clump together and float around in the water. Lots of fish eat it. I gathered these samples from the waters around here."

I picked up a bottle. All I could see was murky brown water with greenish-brown gunk floating on top.

Sheena turned the magnifying glass on the plankton. "Gross," she said.

"Go ahead and take a bottle, Billy," Dr. D. suggested. "Feed some to your goldfish. They'll love it."

"Thanks, Dr. D." Clutching the bottle, I headed down the passageway to my cabin.

As I pushed open the door, I said, "Hello, little fish faces. I've got a delicious surprise for you!"

But the fish had a bigger surprise for me. Way bigger.

I stared at the fishbowl. And nearly dropped the bottle of plankton.

Then I screamed, "NO!"

I burst out of my cabin. "Help! Help! Dr. D.!" I cried.

"There's a head — *someone's head* — in my fishbowl!"

6

Dr. D. and Sheena hurried out of the lab. I glanced back at my cabin door, and — *oof!* — slammed right into Sheena.

"Ow!" she whined. "Watch it, Billy!"

"Billy, what's wrong?" asked Dr. D.

"A head!" I gasped, pointing frantically to my cabin.

I struggled to breathe. My stomach lurched. "Oh, wow. Oh, wow. There — there's a human head in my fishbowl!"

Dr. D. frowned and charged into my room. Sheena and I followed.

He pushed open the door . . . and stopped short with a gasp.

"See!" I shouted.

The head stared at us, eyes open, through the glass.

How could Dr. D. and Sheena stand to look at it? It was making me sick. I gulped and turned away.

Sheena giggled.

Giggled?

"What's the matter with you, Sheena?" I demanded. "What's so funny?"

She crossed the room and reached into the fishbowl.

"Sheena, no!" I warned. "Don't touch it!"

Sheena laughed — and lifted the head out by the hair. Then she waved the head, dripping with water.

"Oh, nooooo!" I groaned. I stared at the head in horror.

I could see it clearly now. I could see that it wasn't a human head after all.

It was a large doll's head.

"Got you back!" Sheena taunted. "Got you back for all the tricks you've been playing on me all summer!"

Dr. D. grinned. "You almost fooled me too," he confessed. "The water in the fishbowl made the doll's head look bigger than it really is. Good one, Sheena."

"Thanks, Dr. D." Sheena took a little bow.

My face felt hot. I knew I was blushing. I was so embarrassed. It just isn't like me to fall for such a stupid joke!

Besides, *I'm* supposed to be the joker. Not Sheena.

I stared into the tank. Something was missing.

"Hey!" I said. "Where are my goldfish? And where's my snail?"

Sheena shrugged. I grabbed her by the neck. "What did you do with them?"

"Okay, okay, don't worry," she said. She pushed me away. "I put them in a smaller bowl and left them in the bathroom."

"Well, get them!" I insisted. I was really angry.

"I'm going, I'm going," Sheena said. She brought my fish and my snail back, and I gently returned them to their bowl.

"Don't ever touch them again!" I told my sister. "I don't want anything to happen to them."

I watched the fish swim around for a minute. They didn't look right. I shook my head. "Something's the matter with them," I said.

"Give them a little plankton, Billy," Dr. D. suggested. "That ought to perk them right up."

I grabbed the glass bottle and pulled off the stopper. I poured a little of the slimy gunk into the bowl.

The fish darted to the surface and started eating. They looked much happier.

"Wow," I said. "They love it!"

"I thought they would." Dr. D. smiled, but his eyes clouded over with worry. "Now, kids, no more jokes, please. I'm going back to the lab to examine that giant minnow. And I don't want to be disturbed."

"We'll be quiet," Sheena promised.

Dr. D. hardly seemed to hear her. "There's something strange going on here," he murmured. "Something very, very strange . . . "

Little did we know that things were about to get much stranger.

7

I paced the deck, thinking hard. I was dying to get Sheena back for that stupid doll trick.

She seemed nervous the rest of the afternoon. Waiting for me to strike.

But I hadn't thought of anything good enough. I'd spent all night thinking, until I fell asleep.

Now it was the next day. Sheena's guard was down. Maybe she'd forgotten — forgotten that *she'd* been the last one to play a trick on me.

And now it was her turn to be fooled.

What would make her hair stand on end? I wondered. What would scare her so much, she'd scream her head off?

The shark trick with the pillow had backfired. So I really owed her *two* tricks.

Maybe I could leave something gross in her bed?

The morning sun beat down on me. Summer

days were hot in the Caribbean. I started to get a headache.

But I finally thought of something good to do to Sheena.

I grabbed my snorkeling gear and pulled it on. I decided to sneak off and explore a little.

Dr. D. wanted us to stay close to the boat. But he didn't want to be disturbed. So snorkeling seemed like a good idea.

Mask and snorkel in place, I started down the boat ladder.

"Caught you!"

Sheena's squeaky voice pierced my eardrums. She was always catching me doing something.

"Where are you going?" she demanded. "Dr. D. said to stay close."

"I won't go far," I insisted. "I'm hot and I'm bored. I can't sit on deck another second."

"Then I'm coming with you." She snatched up her gear and started tugging it on.

I dropped off the ladder and into the water. She slipped in beside me.

"We shouldn't be doing this," she whispered. "What if that shark comes back?"

"The shark is gone," I said. "Don't worry. Nothing bad will happen."

"Promise?" she asked, pulling down her mask.

"Yeah. Sure. I promise," I said.

It was a peaceful, sunny day. The waves were as gentle as a lake. What could happen?

Sheena and I swam out over the sunlit, gleaming water. We thought we'd see lots of pretty little fish.

We found something else. Something we never expected in a million years.

8

I dunked Sheena's head under the water. When she popped back up for air, I shouted, "Shark! Shark!"

Sheena clonked me on the head with her fist. "Don't even joke about it, Billy." Still, I caught her glancing around nervously.

I scanned the horizon too. No signs of a fin anywhere.

A school of lemon-yellow fish drifted by, glowing like little suns in the water. Swimming slowly, I followed them to the coral reef.

Wow, I thought. The coral made a cool shape at that spot. The fish swam through a big pink ring of coral and around a pointy coral peak.

Sunlight filtered down on it through the water. It looked like the tower of a magic sand castle.

A tiny crab popped out of one of the holes in the coral tower. It saw me coming and disappeared.

The yellow fish suddenly rose to the surface, up to a plankton bed that floated on top of the water.

The plankton looked just like the stuff Dr. D. kept in those bottles in his lab.

I watched the fish nip at the plankton, just as my goldfish did.

I surfaced and spit my snorkel out.

"Sheena, check this out," I called.

No answer.

"Sheena?"

I saw a splash on the other side of the reef. Another splash.

I glimpsed Sheena's flippers as they slapped the water.

I swam after her. She had her head down, snorkeling. She must have been watching something very closely. She swam fast, kicking her fins in a rapid, steady rhythm.

"Sheena!" I called again. She couldn't hear me.

She wouldn't hear me if I swam up beside her and screamed. She's like that sometimes. Like when she does her homework. She gets so into it, she blocks everything else out.

Of course she gets straight A's. My mom and dad are constantly bragging about it.

I sighed and paddled after her. I had to go get her. She was swimming out to sea without even realizing it.

I watched her through my mask as I swam. What was that up ahead of her? A patch of cloudy water?

Whoa. No. Not water. I'd never seen anything like it before.

Sheena didn't seem to see it. She was swimming steadily, straight for it.

And, to my horror, it began to move!

I blew water from my snorkel tube and squinted hard through my mask. The thing drifted closer. It was pink and rubbery. Like a soft blob of bubblegum.

It billowed toward Sheena.

And as I stared at it, it appeared to stretch.

It billowed and stretched, billowed out like a pink parachute. Until it was bigger than Sheena.

What is that thing? I wondered. Sheena, turn around! Didn't she see it? Didn't she see it expanding, curling out, stretching in front of her?

"Sheena! Turn around! Turn around!"

I wanted to shout. But I couldn't shout underwater.

I thrashed hard. Kicked. Spun around. Desperate to get her attention.

Sheena! — turn around! I thought. Get away from that thing! Get away — now!

But she kept her head down. And swam straight into the billowy pink blob.

And as I stared on helplessly, it wrapped itself around her. Like an enormous pink clam, it opened wide . . . wider . . . and slipped itself around her.

Held her. Held her tight. Pulled her inside.

And swallowed her.

9

For a moment, I froze in terror.

Then I pulled myself to the surface. Tossed off the mask. And started to swim toward her.

I splashed across the water, racing toward the pink blob. It writhed and wriggled with my sister inside it.

What is it? I wondered. What can it be?

And then, as I pulled myself closer, I knew what it was.

I was staring at a jellyfish!

A jellyfish bigger than a human.

Whoa!

I could see through it. I saw the white, filmy slime and the red veins that made it look pink.

And Sheena — trapped inside!

Poor Sheena. Squirming. Kicking. Slapping at the gooey pink sides of the creature.

Her face pushed up against the veiny jellyfish

skin! Through her mask, I saw her eyes wide with terror.

The ugly creature wrapped around her like a slimy blanket, covering her whole body.

She pushed both fists against the filmy, pink curtain.

I knew she didn't have much air left in her lungs.

I had to do something. But what?

Sheena's face twisted in panic.

I'll have to pry it open somehow, I decided.

I swam up to the wriggling blob. I tried to grab its side.

Ugh! My hands slid right off.

I grabbed for it again. No way. I couldn't get a grip on it. It was like squeezing Jell-O.

Its skin slapped against me, so slimy and sticky.

Sheena stared out at me, eyes bulging with terror.

I tried to wrestle the ugly creature. I dug my fingernails into it.

It wriggled and throbbed. But it didn't open.

Then I realized what I had to do.

The thought made me want to puke. But I knew I had no other choice.

Sheena couldn't hold out much longer.

I had to slide inside the jellyfish myself. I had to get in there somehow and pull Sheena out.

I swallowed.

My stomach lurched.

I lowered my head and dove for the seam, the opening where the disgusting pink blob had folded itself in half.

Here goes! I told myself.

I'm going inside. . . .

10

I worked my hands inside first. Then I lowered my head and pulled myself in.

The slime oozed across my face. The red veins rubbed my skin raw.

I held my breath and worked my way toward Sheena's feet. If I could make it halfway in and grab her feet, maybe I could yank her out.

The blob pulsed, sucking me deep inside. I inched in, stretching toward Sheena's foot.

My lungs were ready to burst. I couldn't hold my breath much longer.

Closer, closer . . .

Aha! My fingers closed around Sheena's flipper!

I tugged. Hard.

Harder.

She started to move.

No.

Oh, no!

Sheena's flipper. It came off in my hand.

I let go of the flipper and reached up a little higher. I grabbed her foot. And tugged.

Sheena slipped down a little.

I yanked on her foot again. Come on! I thought. Move!

But this time Sheena didn't budge.

The sticky pink skin tightened around us. My insides felt as if they were about to explode!

The jellyfish squeezed us tighter and tighter.

It was squeezing us to death!

11

I couldn't move. My mind raced.

How can I get out of here? How?

There was no way. We were doomed!

I'm going to black out, I realized. Another second without air, and . . .

Suddenly, the jellyfish loosened its grip. With a horrible sucking noise, it peeled apart.

It opened!

I didn't waste time. I grabbed Sheena and hauled her up. Up, up, to the surface.

We burst out of the water, gasping for air.

We made it!

I sucked in a huge gulp of air. Aahh. It was great to breathe again.

The blue faded from Sheena's face as the color came back to her cheeks.

"Are you okay?" I asked her.

She nodded, still struggling to catch her breath.

"You sure? Can you talk?"

She nodded again. "Yes, Billy. I'm just great. I've never been better."

I knew she was fine. Her old smart-mouth was working perfectly.

"What happened?" I cried. "Why did the jelly-fish let us go?"

Sheena shrugged. We peered down through the clear water.

The jellyfish floated a few feet below us. And as we stared down at it, we saw why it forgot about us.

We saw *another* enormous pink shape slither and slide toward the first one.

It stretched out in the water as if spreading its wings.

And then it tried to wrap the other jellyfish in-side it.

The two ugly creatures slapped together. The collision sent up a wave that tossed Sheena and me back.

When I gazed down again, they were wrestling. Folding into each other. Slapping and twisting. Struggling to fold the other inside. To swallow it whole.

Another sticky slap. Another.

As they struggled, the water churned and swirled.

The jellyfish monsters broke apart and slammed into each other again. Huge waves churned up around us.

"We've got to get back to the boat!" I yelled.

A wave slapped the side of my head. I choked and spit out a mouthful of seawater.

We struggled to swim against the waves, but they kept knocking us down and pulling us out to sea.

The water was so white and foamy, we couldn't see the jellyfish fight anymore. But we could feel them.

Another wave crashed down on us. I glanced around. "Sheena!"

She was gone!

I frantically searched through the foam. "Sheena!"

Had she gone under?

CRASH! Another wave.

"Sheena, where are you?" I wailed.

She popped up at last, sputtering and choking. I grabbed her and battled against the waves. I fought my way out of the wake of the jellyfish fight.

A few seconds later, Sheena and I dragged ourselves aboard the *Cassandra.*

"That was so weird," Sheena said after we both had caught our breaths. "Those jellyfish — they were as big as cars!"

"We've got to tell Dr. D. about this — right away!" I exclaimed.

We ran down to the lab. No sign of Dr. D. there.

"Dr. D.!" I called. "Where are you?"

"I'll check the galley," Sheena said.

I hurried to see if my uncle was in his cabin. No. The tiny room stood empty.

"He's not in the galley!" Sheena cried. "I don't see him anywhere!"

"Dr. D.!" I shouted. "Dr. D.!"

No reply.

Sheena's chin quivered. I knew she was scared.

It was impossible. But true.

"He-he's gone!" I cried.

12

A pang ripped through my stomach. Dr. D. had just — vanished!

Sheena and I were alone in the middle of the sea!

"What are we going to do?" I asked softly.

"Don't panic," Sheena said. But her voice shook. "Think. Where could he go? Know what? Maybe he just went for a swim."

"A swim? A swim?" I cried, my voice rising. "We probably would have seen him! Besides, since when does Dr. D. just go for a swim? Never!"

"Well — there's always a first time," Sheena suggested. Her eyes darted around nervously. I could see her thinking, trying to stay calm.

"Maybe he went out in the dinghy," she suggested. Dr. D. kept a small boat on deck for short trips. "Let's see if it's gone. Maybe he went out to look for us."

"Good idea." At least it was something. A little hope to cling to.

We hurried up to the deck. I crossed my fingers, hoping to find the dinghy gone.

If the little boat was gone, that meant Dr. D. was probably okay. He'd be back soon.

But if the dinghy was still tied to the deck, and Dr. D. wasn't on the *Cassandra* . . .

Then what?

I raced to the back deck and around to the right —

"Oh, no." I sighed.

The dinghy sat in its usual spot. Dr. D. hadn't taken it out.

"Billy, I'm scared," Sheena whispered.

I was scared too, but I didn't want to admit it. Not yet, anyway.

"Let's check every cabin again," I suggested. "Maybe he's in the bathroom or something. Maybe he didn't hear us calling him."

Sheena followed me down the stairs that led below-deck. Halfway down, the railing rattled in my hand.

"Cut it out, Sheena," I snapped.

"Cut what out?" she cried.

Now the whole stairway shook.

What was she doing? Jumping up and down?

I turned around to check. She stood perfectly still.

"See! I'm not doing anything!"

The boat shook and tilted.

I clutched the rail to keep from falling over.

"What's happening?" I cried.

13

"It's an earthquake!" Sheena shrieked.

"How can it be an earthquake?" I told her. "We're on the water — remember?"

We ran down the steps. The boat tilted, and we both banged hard into the cabin wall.

We passed the lab. The bottles of plankton rattled in the cabinet. Everything rattled. I heard glasses breaking in the galley.

I turned down the passage to my cabin — but I couldn't get by. Something blocked my path.

Something . . .

"*YAAAIIII!*" A scream escaped my throat before I could stop it.

"What *is* that thing?" I cried.

Sheena caught up to me. "Huh? What thing?"

And then she saw it too. It was hard to miss!

"A monster!"

A big creature blocked the passage. It was shiny and black and smooth. And almost perfectly round. It sat in a disgusting puddle of thick white slime.

I'd never seen anything like it before.

Except — something about it looked familiar.

"What *is* it?" Sheena choked out.

The monster stirred. It shook.

And then its head poked out. Long, dripping, and gray — like an enormous slug. With two antennas sticking out of the top.

"Billy" — Sheena grabbed my sleeve — "It's — I think it's a snail!"

"You're right," I muttered in shock. "It *is* a snail. A gigantic, monster snail!"

"How did it get on the boat?" Sheena demanded.

"How did it grow so big?" I added. "It's blocking the entire passage!"

Slowly, slowly, the snail lifted its slimy head. It trained its big, sad, watery eyes on us — and moaned.

"Help me! Help me!" it cried.

14

"*YAAIIII!*" Sheena screamed, and clutched my hand.

I screamed back. "It's talking!"

"Kids! Help!" the snail moaned again.

"Nooooooo! It's talking! It's talking! It's so gross!"

"Billy, calm down!" the snail scolded. "Stop screaming! I need . . . help!"

Sheena and I both gasped.

We both realized the snail wasn't talking. It was Dr. D.!

"I'm trapped. Under the snail!" he choked out. "Can't breathe. Get me out. Hurry."

Dr. D.'s hand waved weakly from under the big snail. His fingers were dripping with the thick white slime.

"The slime — it's as thick as shaving cream!" I murmured.

"Kids, hurry! Can't breathe under here! The slime . . . going up my nose!"

"What should we do, Dr. D.?" Sheena asked.

He didn't reply.

"He's suffocating!" I cried. "He's drowning in snail slime!"

A groan floated out from under the monstrous snail shell.

"We've got to hurry!" Sheena cried.

"I'll tilt the snail over," I told Sheena. "You pull Dr. D. out."

"Okay."

Dr. D. moaned.

"We're coming! We're coming!" I cried.

I pushed the shell. It was heavy. It didn't move.

"Try harder, Billy." Sheena stood nearby, ready to grab Dr. D. and pull him out.

I lowered my shoulder and threw my weight against the snail. "It's not budging!"

"I have an idea," Sheena said. "The slime!"

"Huh? What about it?"

"The slime can help us," she explained. She stood behind the snail. "Let's both push the snail from behind. Maybe the slime will make it slide right off him!"

I heard Dr. D. choking under the snail. He was swallowing slime!

I started to gag. But I swallowed hard. Held my breath. Forced the nausea away.

Sheena and I planted our feet behind the snail.

"One, two, three, push!" she yelled.

We threw our weight against the snail. It slid a little bit.

"One more time — go!"

We pushed again.

The snail slowly slid off Dr. D.'s body. It hit the floor with a heavy thud.

Dr. D. slowly climbed to his feet. He was covered with sticky white goop from head to toe.

He coughed and spat out a big glob of slime. "Not tasty," he muttered, shaking his head.

"Dr. D. — what happened?" I asked.

He smeared the gunk from his eyes. "I don't know. All of a sudden, the boat started shaking. I fell down. And the next thing I knew — *BOOM!* — I found this giant snail on top of me!"

I glanced at the snail. It stood quietly in the passageway, oozing slime. Where did it come from? And how did a snail get so big?

"It seemed to come out of thin air," Dr. D. said.

"It looks a lot like the snail in my fishbowl," I offered. "But *my* snail is tiny. It's the size of my fingernail."

"Dr. D.!" Sheena cried. "We saw two gigantic jellyfish! One of them tried to squeeze me to death!"

"What?" Dr. D. turned to Sheena. "Giant jellyfish? What on earth is going on in these waters?"

The boat lurched.

"Whoa!" I cried out as I lost my balance.

The boat rocked hard to one side. We all slammed against the wall.

"Now what?" Sheena moaned.

"Grab the rail, kids!" Dr. D. shouted. "We're tipping over!"

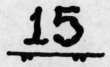

The boat heaved to one side. The huge snail slid across the floor and crashed into the wall.

Tables drifted across the floor. Pictures fell off the walls.

Sheena, Dr. D., and I were pressed against the wall. The boat tilted until we were practically lying down.

"What's happening?" Sheena cried.

Crash! My cabin door flew open. Something thudded heavily inside.

"What was that?" I asked. "Something's going on in my cabin!"

BOOM, BOOM, BOOM. I heard a heavy pounding sound from my room.

"What on earth — ?" Dr. D. murmured.

Sheena gulped. "It sounds like some kind of monster!"

BOOM, BOOM, BOOM.

"I'm going to check it out," I said.

I tried to stand, but the tilt of the boat kept me pinned to the wall.

"I can't get up!" I complained.

Sheena slid along the wall. "Try sliding!"

I inched along the passageway. Sheena and Dr. D. slid along behind me.

I came to a closed door — the door to Sheena's cabin. I tried to step around it, but the gravity pull was too strong. I leaned against the door . . .

"Whoa!" It flew open. I was about to fall in!

I grabbed the door frame. Sheena's cabin floor tilted down behind me. It was like being in the fun house at a carnival.

"Hold on, Billy!" Dr. D. said.

The floor tilted like a steep hill. If I let go of the door, I'd slide down the cabin floor. Then I'd have to crawl my way back up to the passage — if I could.

I clung to the door frame. The gravity pulled me into Sheena's room.

"Help!" My feet slipped out from under me. I felt the wood giving way under my fingernails.

"Pull yourself back up!" Dr. D. instructed. "Don't let go!"

I hauled my body uphill and threw myself to the left. I felt my back slap against the passage wall.

I made it. I made it past Sheena's room. Now all I had to do was slide down the passage to my cabin.

BOOM, BOOM, BOOM. The pounding sound again, inside my cabin.

Behind me, Sheena and Dr. D. struggled past the gaping door to Sheena's cabin.

At last I reached my cabin. The pounding grew louder. *BOOM, BOOM, BOOM.*

What was going on in there?

I peered through the doorway.

"My goldfish!" I gasped. "Oh, nooooo!"

16

My goldfish bowl had smashed to the floor. My two fish lay in a puddle, flopping their tails.

At least they *looked* like my goldfish. But there was one difference — one *huge* difference.

My goldfish were gigantic!

They filled my cabin. They were the size of small whales!

Well, maybe not that big. But they were at least as big as me.

BOOM, BOOM, BOOM. They flopped on the floor, their tails pounding into the wood.

"They — they're giants!" I gasped.

"What's going *on?*" Sheena cried. "How did everything get so big?"

"Oh, my. Oh, my!" Dr. D. muttered over and over. "Oh, my!" He seemed to be in shock.

We all stared at the fish. First the minnow, then the snail, and now this. It was hard to believe.

What was happening? Why was everything suddenly growing so huge?

"I feel like I'm living in some kind of dinosaur world," I said. "Only instead of dinosaurs, we're surrounded by giant sea creatures!"

Dr. D. shook his head to clear it. "I've got to get a grip on myself. We've got big problems here!"

"Huge problems!" Sheena added.

"No wonder the boat's tipping over," Dr. D. said. "Those fish are monstrous! Their weight is pulling the boat over."

"My goldfish, my goldfish!" I couldn't believe it.

They looked beautiful, all golden and shiny. You could really see them now that they were so big — nearly as big as horses. Little brown specks on their gills and their scales glittered in the sunlight that spilled through my porthole.

"We've got to get rid of them," Dr. D. said. "Otherwise, they'll tip over the boat."

"Can we shove them through the window?" Sheena asked.

"They're too big," Dr. D. said. "We'll have to haul them up to the deck somehow."

"And then what?" I asked.

"Throw them overboard," Dr. D. declared. "We can't keep them here, that's for sure."

"Maybe they'll be happier in the ocean," Sheena reasoned. "They probably hated being cooped up in that little bowl, anyway."

"But goldfish are freshwater fish!" I protested.

"We have no choice, Billy," Dr. D. said grimly.

"We won't survive out here. We won't be able to sail anywhere — unless we get these giant fish overboard."

I knew he was right. The fish had to go.

"You two grab the tail. I'll push from the other side," my uncle said.

I tugged on the slick golden tail. "Unh — it's so heavy!" I grunted.

The fish flopped. The tail slapped Sheena's hand.

"Ow!" she cried. "That hurt!"

"Hold him still!" Dr. D. ordered.

We dragged the first fish out of my room — uphill — and into the passage. The snail no longer blocked our path. The snail slime in the passage helped us slide it out.

We hauled the big fish up the steps. It flopped on the deck.

"Good-bye, goldfish," I said.

We shoved it overboard. It flipped its tail and swam away.

"Now we have to do it all over again," Sheena complained.

"And what about the snail?" I said. "It's even heavier than these fish!"

"One monster at a time," Dr. D. said.

As soon as we dragged the other fish overboard, the boat righted itself.

"What a relief," Dr. D. said. "I can stand up straight again!"

"I'm beat," Sheena whined. "This has been the worst day of my life."

We started back down below. The boat looked like the set of a disaster movie. Broken glass everywhere, pools of water, floors and walls streaked with white slime. And the giant snail sitting in the corner.

"What are we going to do about *him*?" Sheena asked.

Dr. D. sighed heavily. "Let's just leave him for now."

I slipped on a puddle of slime on my way to my cabin.

My cabin. What a mess.

It looked as if a giant had come, turned it upside down, and shaken it.

I headed for the closet to get a mop. I stopped.

I thought I heard something.

I listened. Yes. Footsteps. Up on deck.

"Dr. D.?" I called.

"Right here, Billy," he answered. He was busy cleaning up his lab.

Sheena popped out of her cabin. "Did you hear that?" she asked.

I nodded. "Someone's up on deck."

Dr. D. came out of the lab, wiping his hands on a towel. He glanced at me, then at Sheena. Then he looked up toward the ceiling.

"If we're all down here," he began, "then who's walking around up there?"

We crept up the stairs and stepped out on deck.
The afternoon sun beat down on us.

"I don't see anyone," I said.

"Look behind you," boomed a deep voice.

We turned around.

There stood three men. Three total strangers.

17

The three men stood side by side, wearing shorts, button-down shirts, and boating shoes.

The man who had spoken was tall and thin, with glasses and longish brown hair. On his left stood a burly, sunburned blond man. On the right, a curly-haired guy with a long, beaky nose on a birdlike face.

I'd never seen any of them before. What were they doing on our boat?

Dr. D. cleared his throat. "May I help you?"

The tall man spoke. "I hope we didn't frighten you. And I'm sorry to barge aboard like this, but we were worried. Are you in trouble? We saw your boat tilting dangerously to one side and became alarmed."

Dr. D. chuckled, trying to act casual. "We hit some rough water," he lied. "But everything is all right now, as you can see."

Where did these guys come from? I wondered. I

stepped to the edge of the deck and saw a motor-boat tied up to the side.

"I was afraid you were going to tip over," the man said. "We thought we would have to rescue you!"

"No, no. We're fine now. Aren't we, kids?" Dr. D. insisted.

"Fine?" I blurted out. "What about —"

Dr. D. squeezed my shoulder. Hard. I shut my mouth.

Why was Dr. D. acting as if everything were okay?

When goldfish blow up into monsters, every-thing is *not* okay.

"It was very kind of you to come and help." Dr. D. let go of my shoulder, finally. I rubbed it.

"My pleasure." The tall man smiled. "I'm glad there's no trouble. Always happy to help a fellow sailor."

He offered his right hand. "I'm Dr. Ritter. These are my assistants, Mel Mason and Adam Brown." Mel was the burly blond one. Adam was the curly-haired beaky one.

Dr. D. shook his hand. "Nice to meet you. I'm Dr. George Deep. This is my nephew, Billy, and my niece, Sheena."

"Hi, kids. Wow, they look like good, strong swimmers."

Dr. D. grinned. "They are."

"What kind of doctor are you, Dr. Deep?" Dr. Ritter asked. "A surgeon on vacation?"

Dr. D. shook his head. "No. I'm a marine biologist. The *Cassandra* is my floating lab."

"Really?" he asked. "A fellow scientist! Wonderful!"

Dr. Ritter began to stroll around the deck, gazing at the ropes and equipment. His assistants followed him.

"I've got a floating lab myself," Dr. Ritter told us. "Not far from here, as a matter-of-fact."

He sucked in a big breath of salty air and patted his chest. "Ah, yes. We marine biologists are a noble bunch, don't you think, Dr. Deep? Studying the mysteries of the sea. It's the last true frontier on earth, I always say."

Dr. D. trailed after him. "Yes. The last frontier," he agreed.

"What are you working on, if I may ask?" Dr. Ritter said.

Dr. D. cleared his throat. "Oh, I've got a couple of projects going. I can't really talk about them now, Dr. Ritter. They're in their early stages. I'm sure you understand."

The three strangers paused by the ladder where their boat was tied.

"Yes. Indeed. I guess we should be leaving," Dr. Ritter said. "I'm glad you're all safe."

"Thanks for stopping to help," Dr. D. said.

Dr. Ritter put his hand on the ladder. Then he stopped.

"By the way — you haven't seen anything strange in the waters around here lately, have you?"

"Strange?" Dr. D. asked. "What do you mean?"

"Odd fish, unusual creatures, anything like that?"

Odd fish! I couldn't hold it in any longer. "We've seen all kinds of weird stuff!" I gushed. "My gold-fish turned into giants! And we saw huge jellyfish bigger than a car! Ow!"

Something sharp poked me in the ribs. My uncle's elbow.

Whoops.

"I'm sorry to hear that," Dr. Ritter said.

"Yes, it was really scary!" I agreed. "Ow!" Dr. D.'s elbow again. "What did you do that for?"

He frowned at me.

What? I thought. What did I do this time?

"Billy is just joking," Dr. D. assured him. He played nervously with his glasses.

Dr. Ritter said, "Joking? You weren't really joking — were you, Billy?"

"Well . . ." I gazed up at Dr. D. I didn't know what to say.

"I'm really sorry," Dr. Ritter repeated. "I'm sorry you saw those creatures, Billy. Because now I can't let you go."

"Huh?" I gasped. "What are you talking about?"

"You've seen too much," Dr. Ritter replied solemnly. "And now I have to decide what to do with you."

He snapped his fingers. The two assistants moved in.

18

"Hold on, there." Dr. D. put his arms around me and Sheena. "Don't pay any attention to Billy. He has a wild imagination."

"The wildest," Sheena piped in.

"He's always making up stories," Dr. D. went on.

"He's a big fat liar," Sheena added. "Everybody knows that."

"Believe me, Dr. Ritter," my uncle pleaded. "We haven't seen anything strange at all. I mean, a giant goldfish? You're a scientist, Dr. Ritter. You know as well as I do that that is impossible."

Dr. Ritter opened his mouth to speak. Something stopped him. A loud noise. A loud, lumbering, thudding sound.

CRASH! PLOP!

Something broke through the doors and bounced onto the deck.

The giant snail.

I dropped my head in my hands. "Oh, no!"

Dr. Ritter raised an eyebrow. "Looks like your brother is not the big fat liar you say he is."

"Oh, he's a big fat liar, all right," Sheena insisted. "And he's stupid too."

I kicked her in the shins.

"Ow!" she cried.

"Kids, quiet!" Dr. D. commanded.

The burly blond guy grabbed me. He pinned my arms behind my back with one hand and gripped me around the neck with the other.

"Let go of me!" I shrieked. "That hurts!"

"Quiet — or I'll really hurt you!" the blond guy threatened.

The beaky guy grabbed Sheena. She squirmed and tried to kick him. But he was too strong for her.

"Let them go!" Dr. D. cried.

Mel tightened his grip on me.

"I'm so sorry, Dr. Deep," Dr. Ritter said. "I hate to harm a fellow scientist. But you shouldn't have snooped around here. I hate snoops."

He sighed. "What a shame you wandered into my plankton beds. What a shame you poked your nose into my experiments."

"What experiments?" Dr. D. asked.

Dr. Ritter laid a strong hand on Dr. D.'s shoulder. "I'm working on such a brilliant project. It could change the world. It could solve all our problems!"

"What is it?"

"Ha-ha. You *are* a curious fellow!" Dr. Ritter laughed. "Well, I may as well tell you. I've been injecting a growth hormone into the plankton beds in these waters. The fish who feed on the plankton grow to be very large. You've seen the results yourself."

Dr. D. nodded. "But how does that solve any problems?"

"In my heart, I'm a good man," Dr. Ritter said. "I don't want to hurt anyone. I want to help *everyone*! I plan to raise huge fish to feed the world. No one will ever have to go hungry!"

"Let go of me!" Sheena screamed. Adam still held her tightly.

"This one is noisy," Adam complained.

"Let her go," Dr. Ritter said. "For now."

Adam dropped his arms. But he stayed right behind Sheena.

"Your experiments sound interesting, Dr. Ritter," my uncle said. "I'd like to hear more. Are they working?"

Dr. Ritter smiled. I could tell he liked to talk about his work. "Well, there are a few kinks at the moment. But nothing I can't fix."

"What are you going to do with us?" Sheena broke in.

Dr. Ritter frowned at her. "I'm afraid you know too much."

"But I am a scientist," Dr. D. declared. "I would

never tell anyone about your work. You have my word on that."

"Your word isn't enough," Dr. Ritter growled. His temper flared. His face reddened. "I can't let anyone steal my idea."

"I would *never* steal!" my uncle insisted.

"I'll make sure of that," the other scientist replied coldly. He turned to his two assistants. "Take them."

Before Sheena or I could move, Mel and Adam grabbed us and forced us into their motorboat.

I broke away for a second. And scrambled for the ladder, trying to get back to the *Cassandra*.

But before I could reach it, they grabbed Dr. D. and forced him aboard their boat too.

Mel cut the line with one flick of a knife. Adam started the motor.

It all happened so fast. We didn't have a chance.

Dr. Ritter jumped aboard and grabbed the wheel. He steered the boat out to sea.

"Where are you taking us?" I cried. "What are you going to do?"

19

"Get down there!" Adam shoved Dr. D. down into the small cabin. Sheena and I stumbled after him. Mel followed behind us.

"What are you going to do?" I repeated.

"You'll see," Adam growled.

We marched through a tiny galley. Mel and Adam forced us through a small door into a stuffy cabin with a table and chairs. Mel tied Dr. D. to a chair.

"This really isn't necessary," my uncle said softly. I could see he was trying to sound calm.

"Tell that to Dr. Ritter," Mel muttered.

Adam tied up Sheena, then me.

"Not so tight!" I cried. I leaned over and bit Adam's arm.

"Good one, Billy!" Sheena bounced in her chair.

"Hey!" Adam pulled back, rubbing his arm. "This kid bit me!"

"Bite him back," Mel muttered.

Adam bared his teeth at me. But he didn't bite me. And he didn't tighten my ropes.

My plan worked. I was tied to the chair — but not as tightly as he thought.

Mel and Adam studied us. "Okay. We've taken care of them," Mel said. "Let's go get some lunch."

They left the cabin, shutting the door behind them. I could hear them in the little galley, rattling plates and silverware.

I glanced out the porthole to my right. The boat was speeding away, far from the *Cassandra*. Out to sea.

I jiggled my hands, trying to loosen the ropes. They were tied pretty well. If I could just get the rope to stretch a little . . .

"What could this guy Ritter be up to?" Dr. D. wondered out loud. He wasn't really talking to me and Sheena. He was figuring things out for himself.

"This plankton he's invented really does make fish grow bigger," he said. "It could help end hunger in the world."

"Isn't that good, Dr. D.?" Sheena asked.

I rubbed my wrists against the ropes. Come on, loosen, I thought.

"It might be good," Dr. D. went on. "But it could be bad too. It could throw the whole balance of nature off."

Rub, rub, rub. I tested the ropes. Were they a little looser?

"I mean, what are these giant fish supposed to eat? More and more plankton? They might eat up all the little fish. They might even start eating *people*. Who knows?"

I stretched my hands against the ropes. The knot had loosened! I tried to pull one of my hands through.

No. Still too tight.

"And Dr. Ritter mentioned some kinks," my uncle continued. "Some problems. I wonder what he was talking about. It could be anything."

I strained to hear what Mel and Adam were doing in the galley. It sounded as if they had taken their lunch up on deck.

I yanked the ropes hard. I felt something give.

I squeezed one hand through the rope. The knot burned against my skin.

Pulling, pulling . . .

I got it out! One hand was free!

"Dr. D.!" I whispered. I held up my free hand.

"Good going, Billy!" he whispered back.

I untied my other hand and leaped up to untie my uncle.

"Billy, hurry!" Sheena urged me. "Maybe we can sneak off the boat!"

Then the door flew open.

"You interrupted my lunch," Dr. Ritter said, shaking his head. "That's not very polite."

He blocked the doorway. Mel and Adam planted themselves beside him.

64

"You want to get off the boat?" he asked. "That can be arranged. Mel, Adam. Take them on deck!" he ordered.

Mel and Adam untied Sheena and Dr. D. and dragged us upstairs. Dr. Ritter's lunch — sandwiches, a salad — sat half eaten on a table.

The two men herded us to the side of the boat. I looked down.

The ocean churned beneath us. No other boats, not a patch of land in sight.

No one, nothing to save us.

Nothing but sea — endless, deep sea.

And gigantic, hungry, sea creatures.

"Which one of you will jump first?" Dr. Ritter asked. "Or do you all want to go together?"

I gazed down at the thrashing waves. Then I took a deep breath —

And got ready to jump.

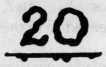

20

The waves crashed beneath me. My heart pounded so hard, it hurt.

I sucked in a lungful of air. This could be my last breath, I realized.

"Stop!" Dr. D. cried. "Let me jump, Ritter. Spare the kids. They can't harm you or your experiments."

"I think a family should stick together," Dr. Ritter said. "Especially a family of snoops."

"We're not snoops!" Sheena protested. "We can't help it if we accidentally saw some of your big fish!"

"We won't tell anyone about them! Really!" I cried.

Dr. Ritter leaned close to Sheena. "Perhaps *you* would like to go first?"

Sheena glared at him, but I saw her shaking. I knew she was really scared. And Sheena hardly ever gets scared.

"Leave her alone," Dr. D. warned. "Take us to

an island — any island. Whatever is nearest. Then we won't be able to tell anyone about your plankton experiments."

Dr. Ritter scowled. "There are no islands nearby. And I can't take the chance. Sorry."

Dr. D. refused to give up. He kept trying to stall, to talk his way out of this.

But there was no way. I could see that.

Think! Think! I ordered myself desperately. There's got to be some way to escape. There's got to be.

I glanced around, searching for something, *anything*. Maybe a life jacket! Didn't they have life jackets on the boat? Or a floating ring?

If I could grab some kind of float, at least we'd have a chance.

But I didn't see anything on the deck. I craned my neck to look back at the stern.

My heart beat faster. Yes! A rubber lifeboat.

"What are you looking at, kid?" Mel growled. "You looking for the coast guard or something? Believe me, there's no one around to rescue you so forget about it."

"I — I wasn't looking at anything," I stammered. I was so scared, I could hardly breathe.

"Enough of this stalling around," Dr. Ritter interrupted. "You're wasting my time. And you're wasting your breath. And you're going to need all the breath you've got. It's time for a swim."

Sheena let out a scream.

"Let her go," Dr. D. shouted.

Two strong hands gripped my shoulders.

"Help!" I shrieked. "Please — no!"

But screaming did no good.

They pushed me over the side.

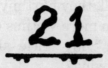

21

I shut my eyes and prepared for the cold shock of the water.

But I didn't fall.

The strong hands didn't let go.

I felt myself pulled back into the boat — as a dark shadow swept overhead.

"Huh?" I blinked several times. Was it a shadow — or my eyes?

I heard a deafening noise. A clattering. A beating sound.

I turned to Dr. D. He and the others all had their eyes on the sky.

A helicopter? I thought. Is it a helicopter? Someone to rescue us?

No. That clapping, pounding sound couldn't be a helicopter's roar.

Another shadow swooped over the boat.

And then an ugly cry ripped through the air.

RRRAAAAAK! RRAAAAAAK!

"Oh, no!" Dr. D. cried. "Here they come!"

I shielded my eyes with one hand. And I saw them.

Swooping low. Two enormous birds. Seagulls. Seagulls as big as my golden Lab back home!

RRRAAAAAK! RRAAAAAK! Their sharp cries were so shrill, they hurt my ears.

"Here come two more victims of your great experiments, Ritter," my uncle shouted over the pounding of their wings.

"They must have eaten the plankton too!" Dr. Ritter exclaimed.

The birds circled the boat. They cast huge shadows over us, their wings stretched out like sails.

As I squinted up at them, they stopped circling.

And lowered their talons.

Are they hunting for food? I wondered, staring up at the sharp bird claws, gleaming in the sunlight.

Are *we* the food?

Before we could duck or try to hide, the two huge birds soared toward us.

Talons raised. Ready to clutch their prey.

Screeching all the way down.

22

I froze in panic.

The screeching rang in my ears. Filled my brain. Made me feel as if my head would burst.

I stared up at the raised talons.

The shadows of the screeching birds washed over me.

And then I felt a strong hand pushing me down. Down to the deck. I turned back and saw my uncle, his jaw set, his eyes on the sky.

He pushed Sheena and me down. Then moved over us. Protecting us.

I couldn't see them. But I felt the heavy *thud* as the two heavy gulls landed on the boat.

And then I heard the shouts of Dr. Ritter and his men. Angry shouts, over the shrill squawks of the birds.

I twisted my head. Tried to see. But my uncle pushed my head down again. Holding his arms over Sheena and me.

I heard a struggle behind us. More squawks. More frantic cries.

I heard the heavy pounding of wings.

A table fell over. Dishes crashed to the floor.

A cry of pain.

"Quick, kids — now's our chance!" Dr. D. whispered. He pulled us to our feet. Then, protecting us with his back, he shoved us across the deck to the lifeboat.

"Billy! Help me untie this thing!" Dr. D. ordered.

The three of us struggled with the knots that held the lifeboat to the deck.

"Hurry!" Dr. D. urged us. "Before they see what we're up to!"

"RRRAAAAK!" I turned and saw that one of the birds had Adam pinned under its sharp claws. Mel and Dr. Ritter were struggling to pull the powerful bird off him.

"This knot's undone!" Sheena announced. She worked on another knot.

I nervously tugged at the knot in my hands. I was so scared, I couldn't think. My fingers felt thick and clumsy.

Hurry! I ordered myself. Hurry — before they catch us!

Finally, I ripped open the last knot and pulled the lifeboat free. Dr. D. tossed it into the water, holding it by a rope.

"Okay. Let's go! Jump in! Now!"

I gripped the rail of the motorboat and braced myself to jump.

"Hey!" I heard a cry behind me. I turned back and saw Mel staring at us. "Hey — they're getting away!"

He motioned to us. "Stop!" he shouted. He grabbed a spear gun. "Don't move!" he ordered.

I hesitated. The sharp point of the metal spear sparkled in the sunlight.

Would he really shoot us?

"Go, kids! Now!" Dr. D. cried.

Mel aimed the spear gun at my uncle — and fired.

23

WHOOSH!

I couldn't see it. It moved so fast, I could only *hear* the spear fly through the air.

To my horror, Dr. D. slumped to the deck.

"You — you *shot* him!" I shrieked.

"Dr. D.! Dr. D.!" Sheena cried. We both hurried to his side.

Our uncle sat up.

"It — it missed!" He seemed surprised. He leaped to his feet. "Into the lifeboat, kids!" he cried.

A gull squawked. I heard Adam scream. Mel turned back to help him.

I took a running jump, shut my eyes, and threw myself overboard.

PLOP! I landed in the soft rubber boat. Sheena jumped in after me. Then Dr. D.

"Stop, or I'll shoot!" Dr. Ritter called. He picked up Mel's spear gun and aimed it at us.

A gull's wing bumped his arm, knocking the gun into the water.

We frantically scooped our hands through the water, paddling away from Dr. Ritter's boat.

"You can't escape!" Dr. Ritter called after us, shaking his fist. "I'll get you!"

Dr. D. grabbed the lifeboat paddles. He started paddling with all his strength. The ocean pulled us away.

The ocean turned rough and foamy. A wind kicked up and blasted us, churning up huge waves. The waves carried us quickly out to sea.

Dr. Ritter's boat faded into the distance.

"Well, we escaped," Sheena sighed. "But where are we *going*?"

No sign of land anywhere. No sign of another boat. Nothing but water. Churning water and crashing waves.

The rubber lifeboat smacked down hard on the water. "Hold on, kids," Dr. D. shouted. "Here comes a big one!"

I gripped the sides of the boat as a huge wave tossed us into the air.

THUMP! We landed in a valley between waves. Then another wave smashed over us.

I shivered, totally soaked.

"Is everybody okay?" Dr. D. asked. Sheena and I nodded.

Then a gigantic wave caught us from behind.

The lifeboat bounced high in the air. I clung to the side.

But Sheena's hands slipped off. She flew up into the air— and disappeared into the white foam.

"Sheena!" I screamed. "She fell overboard!"

Her head bobbed up. "H-h-help!" she sputtered. She sank below again, her arms thrashing.

I waited for her to bob back up.

Waited.

Waited.

Please — I prayed.

And then there she was. I leaned over the side. Leaned forward. More. More . . .

And grabbed her arm and hauled her back into the boat.

"Are you all right, Sheena?" Dr. D. asked.

She coughed. Water ran down her face. "I think so."

Dr. D. held on to her as another big wave drenched us.

We huddled in the lifeboat, wet, shivering, hungry, and tired. The lifeboat puddled with water. It was like sitting in a wading pool.

The sky grew dark. It would be night soon.

We'll have to spend the night out here, I realized. Out here in the middle of the ocean.

We can't even rest. The ocean is so rough. If we let go of the boat for a second, we could be thrown into the sea.

We had no food, no water. Nothing.

"It can't get any worse than this, can it?" I demanded. "Can it?"

Sheena sneezed. Dr. D. said nothing.

It can't get any worse, I repeated to myself.

And then it did.

24

The sky darkened to black. Then lightning crackled overhead.

KABOOM!

A roar of thunder shook our tiny lifeboat.

Rain poured down on us. Heavy sheets of cold rain.

"I don't believe this!" Sheena wailed. She wiped strands of wet hair from her face.

We sat glumly in the boat. The waves bounced us. The wind blew across our drenched skin. The rain hammered down on us.

Lightning ripped across the sky.

Dr. D. gazed up at the heavy, low clouds and frowned. "It's not going to let up anytime soon," he announced.

Great.

Meanwhile, the lifeboat filled up with water.

Dr. D. tried to scoop the water out with his hands. "Help me bail, kids!" he ordered. "If the boat fills up too much, we'll sink!"

We furiously scooped the water out. But the rain filled the boat as fast as we could empty it. What were we going to do?

I took off one of my sneakers and tried bailing water with it. It worked better than nothing. So Dr. D. and Sheena used their shoes to bail too.

The rain roared down for hours. "I'm so tired!" I complained. I threw down my shoe. "I can't bail any more water. I can't!"

"Don't give up, Billy," Dr. D. scolded. "We'll make it." He didn't sound as if he really believed it, though.

"Don't worry," he said, shouting over a boom of thunder. "We're going to be all right."

I don't see how, I thought. If we don't starve to death, we'll sink! There's no one around to save us. No one . . .

The rain finally stopped. By then it was night. Totally dark. No moon. No stars. Just a black sky blanketed by clouds.

"I'm so cold," Sheena whined.

"I'm hungry," I added.

"I'm seasick!" Dr. D. admitted.

"I'm all three," I told them. "Plus thirsty, tired, and wet."

We all laughed. What else could we do?

When things get *this* bad, it suddenly seems ridiculous!

We huddled together for warmth. My stomach growled.

But I was so tired . . . so tired. I couldn't keep my eyes open. I fell asleep.

I woke up with a *THUMP*. The boat had hit something.

I opened my eyes. And stared out at a silvery, pale world.

I'm dreaming, I thought. I closed my eyes again.

But then I felt my wet clothes sticking to my skin.

No, I realized. I'm awake.

My eyes flew open. Sheena and Dr. D. sat up, yawning and stretching.

"What's happening?" Sheena murmured.

"The boat's not moving," I realized. "It stopped."

I reached out to touch the water. Instead of water, my fingers sifted through sand.

Dry land!

"Hey!" I cried. "We've landed somewhere!"

The sky lightened a little. The sun was just rising. I could begin to make out where we were.

"Land!" Sheena shouted. She jumped out of the boat. "Hurray! Land! I don't believe it! I don't *believe* it!"

Dr. D. stood up and stretched. "Wow! That feels good."

The sun shone brighter now. I threw myself on the sand. "Bake me, sun!" I sighed.

"I wonder where we are," Dr. D. said softly, gazing around.

"Wherever we are, I hope they've got food," Sheena added.

Our lifeboat had landed on a sandy beach. Up a slope I could see a stand of palm trees. Other than that, nothing. No docks, no boats, no houses.

"No sign of any people," Dr. D. noted. "I'm going to take a look around."

"I'm coming too," I said.

"Me too!" Sheena said.

We followed Dr. D. along the beach. We walked along the edge of the water.

"Look! A coconut tree!" Sheena pointed to a tall tree on the beach. A few coconuts nestled in the sand beneath it.

"Let's open one," she insisted. "I'm starving!"

Dr. D. grabbed a coconut and smashed it against a rock. The coconut split open.

Sheena and I pounced on it. We picked up the broken pieces and chewed the coconut meat.

"Feel better?" Dr. D. asked, sipping coconut milk from the shell.

I wiped the sweet liquid from my chin. "A little," I said. "But I could sure use a hamburger. Make that two. And a double order of french fries with tons of catsup."

"Or a pizza," Sheena added.

"We'll catch some fish later," Dr. D. promised. "We can build a fire and cook them."

We continued our way around the island.

"Maybe we'll find a restaurant," Sheena wished out loud.

But after about ten minutes, Dr. D. groaned. "Oh, no!"

"What is it?" I asked.

"Look." He pointed a few yards down the beach.

Our lifeboat. We were right back where we'd started.

"You mean, that's it?" I asked. "We've seen the whole island in ten minutes?"

"That's it." Dr. D. sighed. "It's tiny."

Sheena sighed too. "I'm still hungry. And I don't want coconuts!"

"Looks as if we've landed on a deserted island," Dr. D. said. "But don't worry. We'll find something to eat."

I touched my face. My skin was hot. The sun had felt so good at first — but now I was getting sunburned.

Another question nagged at me. But I was so hungry, I tried to push it out of my mind.

"Billy, run into that clump of palm trees," Dr. D. ordered. "See if you can find some wood to build a fire."

I wandered into the grove, hunting for something to burn. There wasn't much to be found. Mostly a lot of vines.

And that nagging worry wouldn't go away.

We were stuck on a tiny island, with nothing but a rubber raft.

And I had one question, a question I was afraid to ask out loud:

How were we ever going to get off?

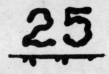

25

I found a few sticks and carried them back to the beach. Dr. D. was digging a pit for the fire.

"Good job, Billy." He took the sticks from me. "This will do for now."

Sheena was wading near the shore. I sat down on the sand. "Dr. D. —" I began. "What are we going to do? Do you think we're far from the *Cassandra*?"

Dr. D. sighed. "I'm afraid I have no idea where we are," he admitted.

"So — what's going to happen? Are we going to rot on this island?" I knew we couldn't last long. So far, we'd had nothing to eat but coconuts.

Dr. D. rubbed two of the sticks together, trying to get them to light. "Maybe someone will see our fire. Maybe a plane will fly over us, or a boat will pass by. Maybe someone will find the *Cassandra* empty and come searching for us."

I leaned back and gazed at the empty sky. "But that could take forever!" I cried. "Nobody even knows we're missing! Except Dr. Ritter — and I don't want *him* to find us."

I heard a shriek. I turned and saw Sheena running up the beach, waving something in one hand.

"Look! Hey — check this out!" she shouted. "I caught a fish! I caught a fish with my bare hands!"

She held out a small, wriggling silverfish.

"It's puny," I said.

"So? Let's see *you* catch one!" she shot back.

Dr. D. took the fish and set it on the sand. "It's better than nothing."

"I'll catch a bigger one," I declared.

Sheena and I raced back to the water. We waded in hip-high. A few small fish darted around us.

"These are all pretty small," I complained. "We need some of Dr. Ritter's plankton to make them grow."

"I wouldn't want to eat one of his giant fish," Sheena replied, making a disgusted face. "Yuck."

"Maybe if we go a little deeper we'll find bigger fish," I suggested.

We waded in farther. A silverfish with a black stripe swam past me.

"That one is a little bigger," I said. I made a grab for it. Missed.

I tried again. I swam out a little farther, chasing the fish.

I guess I waded out deeper than I meant to. Suddenly I felt a sharp pain in my foot.

At first I thought Sheena was pinching me.

But the pain quickly swept up my whole leg.

"Hey — what's going on?" I cried.

I lowered my gaze to the water — and let out a frightened scream.

26

"Oh, nooooo!" I moaned.

I stared down at the water — down at the creature beneath the water.

I saw a hairy back. A brown-purple shell. Enormous pincers.

And knew I'd been grabbed by a giant crab!

The crab was as big as a card table. And it squeezed my toe in a pincer the size of my dad's lug wrench!

"Help!" I screeched. "Ohhhh, help!"

The crab snapped its claws. I managed to slip my toe out of its grip.

Slipping and stumbling, I scrambled back to shore as fast as I could.

"A giant crab!" I shouted. "Hey — look out! It's following me!"

Sheena let out a gasp and came splashing out of the water.

The giant crab scrabbled onto the sand, moving sideways, its hairy legs moving rapidly.

"I don't believe it!" Dr. D. cried.

The crab moved toward us with amazing speed, snapping its claws. *Click . . . click . . . CLICK.*

"Into the trees! Quick!" Dr. D. shouted.

We ran into the palm tree grove. I scrambled up a tree, out of the crab's reach. Sheena climbed up behind me. Dr. D. grabbed the branch of another tree and swung himself up.

The crab watched us from below. It raised its hairy claws as if reaching for us. *Click . . . CLICK.*

"If only we could cook it!" Sheena exclaimed hungrily. "That thing could feed us for a week!"

"It must have eaten some of Dr. Ritter's plankton! Its huge size has made this crab *very* hungry!"

The crab clicked its big claws, trying to grab us. Its body heaved in and out, in and out.

It stood there for what seemed like hours.

"How long will it wait before it gives up?" I asked.

Dr. D. shrugged. "Your guess is as good as mine."

I heard a *crack*.

At first, I thought it was the crab claws snapping.

Another *crack*. Too close to be the crab.

Coming from right beneath Sheena and me.

The tree branch.

Crack.

To my horror, I realized that Sheena and I were too heavy for it. The branch was breaking off the tree.

My sister and I were about to drop into the crab's waiting claws.

27

With a low cry, I reached up both arms. I tried to grab the branch above us.

I reached . . . reached . . .

No. My arms were too short.

"We — we're falling!" Sheena cried.

With a loud *craaaack*, our branch broke off.

And we tumbled down . . . down . . . onto the crab's hairy back.

No.

Onto the hot sand.

"Huh?" I gasped and spun around.

The crab had moved away. It was scrabbling rapidly back toward the water.

Sheena sat up, her expression still startled.

Our uncle climbed down from his branch. "Are you two okay?"

We watched the huge creature splash back into the ocean.

"I'm *never* going back in that water," I declared.

"Who knows what other monsters are waiting in there!"

"But how will we catch any fish?" Sheena wailed. "We're going to starve to death!"

Dr. D. wasn't listening to us. He had turned away and was gazing down the beach. "Oh, no!" he cried. "The tide — it came in! The life raft!"

All three of us started running to the spot where we'd left our lifeboat. But it was gone.

I stared out over the ocean — and I spotted a yellow speck in the distance. The lifeboat.

The tide had carried it away.

"Now we'll never get off this stupid island!" I cried. "Never."

Dr. D. didn't reply. He didn't need to say anything. The worried expression on his face said it all.

We passed the rest of the day keeping in the shade, chewing coconut meat.

"I'll never eat coconut again," Sheena whined. "Not even in candy bars!"

We didn't talk much. What was there to say?

Night fell slowly. We watched the sky fade from blue to purple to black.

Dr. D. sat up suddenly. "Did you hear that?" he asked.

I sat up too. And listened hard.

"What is it?" Sheena asked.

"It's coming from the beach," Dr. D. said.

We walked quickly down to the beach. Two huge animals splashed and played in the water.

"Whales!" Sheena cried.

"No — not whales," Dr. D. said. "Dolphins!"

The dolphins ate the plankton too, I realized.

"What's that yellow thing they're playing with?" Sheena asked. "It looks like —"

"It is!" I shouted. "Our lifeboat! The dolphins brought it back!"

The lifeboat rope had tangled around the middle of one of the dolphins. Wherever the dolphin swam, the boat trailed behind it.

"Let's go rescue it!" Dr. D. cried. He splashed into the water. Sheena and I followed him. No time to worry about giant crabs. We had to get that raft.

We swam out to where the dolphins played. They gurgled at us. They didn't seem afraid of us at all.

Why should they be? They were a lot bigger than we were!

They're only dolphins, I told myself. Dolphins don't hurt people.

But I was a little afraid of them. Especially since our visit from the giant crab.

Dr. D. grabbed the edge of the rubber raft. Sheena and I climbed in.

"Now, if I can just get that rope from around this dolphin . . . ," Dr. D. groaned.

He tugged on the rope. The dolphin began to swim.

"The dolphin is carrying us away!" Sheena said. "Wait, dolphin! Stop!"

The dolphin didn't stop. It kept swimming, faster and harder.

Dr. D. hauled himself into the boat.

The island was a speck behind us now. We couldn't swim back to it if we wanted to! The dolphin was carrying us far out to sea.

"We might as well settle back and enjoy the ride," Dr. D. said. "There's nothing else we can do."

The dolphin pulled us all night long. The sea was calm that night. We slept in the boat again.

When I opened my eyes, everything was gray. Misty.

I heard the dolphin gurgling and chirping, as if it were talking to us.

The sun was just about to come up. The ocean was covered with a thick blanket of fog.

The dolphin poked its head over the side of the boat. It had slipped the rope off. It was free now.

With a splash, it swam away. It quickly disappeared through the thick fog.

I peered through the fog. I could barely see past the lifeboat. We were still in the middle of the ocean. But I thought I saw something nearby. Something big and white.

Like a boat.

My heart sank.

Oh, no, I thought. I think I've seen this boat before.

I shut my eyes again, wishing it would go away.

I opened them. There it was.

No! It can't be! It's too horrible!

I shook Dr. D. "Wake up!" I cried. "Look where we are!"

Dr. D. opened his eyes. "Huh?" my uncle muttered. "Where are we?"

"The dolphin carried us back!" I wailed. "Back to Dr. Ritter's boat!"

28

"Oh, no!" Sheena wailed. "Not again!"

"What are we going to do?" I asked.

"Shhh!" Dr. D. whispered. "Stay calm. They don't know we're here. Maybe we can get away somehow."

"Get away?" I exclaimed. "To where?"

"I can't stay on this raft another minute!" Sheena insisted. "I want to go home!"

"That stupid dolphin!" I muttered. "I thought dolphins were supposed to be smart! I can't believe it pulled us to Dr. Ritter's boat."

The fog surrounded us like a thick gray curtain. It swept in and out, making Dr. Ritter's boat appear to shimmer.

The rubber raft drifted closer to the boat. I could almost touch the side of the bow.

I thought I saw a word printed there. I did. The name of the boat.

I strained to read it. I could make out the first few letters.

C-A-S . . .

Huh?

"Dr. D.!" I cried. "It's not Dr. Ritter's boat. It's *our* boat! It's the *Cassandra*!"

Dr. D. squinted. "Yes!" he cried. "You're right, Billy!"

We were safe! Sheena and I jumped up and danced around.

"We're home! We're home! We're home!" we sang.

The lifeboat bounced under our feet. "Whoa!" I cried. We nearly tipped it over!

"Sit down, kids," Dr. D. said. "We're two feet from safety. We don't want to drown *now*."

We paddled the rubber raft to our boat and dragged ourselves aboard.

I was so tired. But I couldn't help doing another little dance on the deck of the *Cassandra*.

Sheena slapped me five. "Nothing can stop us!" she cried happily. "Not a stormy night on the high seas! Not getting stranded on an empty island! Nothing!"

Dr. D. laughed. "I can't wait to take a shower and go to bed. But first — I'm cooking us all a big breakfast."

"Pancakes!" I suggested.

"Pancakes and waffles!" Sheena cried.

"Breakfast is going to have to wait," a deep voice said.

We all froze.

Dr. Ritter stepped out of the cabin.

"You won't be hungry much longer," he sneered.

29

"I can't take this!" Sheena wailed. Tears formed in her eyes.

"Quiet!" Dr. Ritter snapped.

Dr. D. laid a hand on Sheena's shoulder and shushed her. "Where are your assistants?" he asked Dr. Ritter.

"That's none of your business. I don't need them now. I can take care of you myself," Dr. Ritter replied. "You're all very tired and weak, aren't you? Even you, Dr. D. That's what happens when you don't eat for two days."

I glanced at Dr. D. It was true. He looked exhausted.

"Go ahead," Dr. Ritter went on. "Get back in the lifeboat. I dare you."

My eyes fell on the rubber boat. Dr. Ritter knew what he was doing. I would rather have eaten fish guts with horseradish than get back in that thing.

"What do you want now, Ritter?" Dr. D.'s voice

was tired, but angry. "Why did you wait here for us?"

Dr. Ritter scowled. "I can't let you live. I can't let you tell the world about my plankton."

"We promised we wouldn't tell!" Sheena cried. "Look — cross my heart and hope to die." She crossed her heart and held up her hand, Girl Scout–style.

Dr. Ritter laughed. "You're very amusing. I'm so sorry it has to end this way. Really, I am."

The sun finally burned through the fog. I shivered. I wasn't cold and wet anymore. But Dr. Ritter was giving me chills.

"All of you — down to the lab," Dr. Ritter ordered. "Go!"

He forced us downstairs. Into my uncle's lab.

Dr. Ritter stood in front of the cabinet — the one that held the plankton bottles.

"I believe these are the plankton samples you collected, Dr. Deep," he said. "Am I right?"

Dr. D. nodded.

"Good. You've gathered a lot of my work. You must have been very interested in it."

"Of course I was," Dr. D. said. "I'm a scientist."

"Yes," Dr. Ritter hissed. "You're a scientist. You want to learn more — am I right?"

Dr. D. nodded slowly.

"Excellent. You asked me earlier about the side effects of my plankton experiments, Dr. Deep.

About the few kinks I haven't worked out yet. I think now is the time to show you what they are."

Dr. Ritter opened the glass door of the cabinet. "When fish eat the plankton, they grow huge." He pointed to the bottles of plankton lined up on the shelves.

"You've already seen that, haven't you? But what do you think happens when a *human* eats the plankton? Billy? Want to take a guess?" Dr. Ritter asked.

I took a stab at it. "Um — they grow into giant people?"

"Wrong!" Dr. Ritter cried. "Sheena? What do you think?"

Sheena shrugged. "I couldn't care less."

"You should care, Sheena," Dr. Ritter said. "Because whatever happens, it's going to happen to *you*."

He turned to my uncle. "Dr. Deep? Any guesses? Or have you already figured it out in your research?"

"Just tell us what happens, Ritter," Dr. D. snapped impatiently.

"All right. I'll tell you. When a human eats the plankton, he turns into a fish!"

"Excuse me?" I cried.

"Is this fairy-tale time?" my uncle groaned.

Dr. Ritter ignored us. "The human becomes a fish!" he repeated. "Almost instantly! And that person will remain a fish — for the rest of his life."

"That's impossible!" Dr. D. protested. "You're crazy, Ritter. Let us take you to shore and get you some help."

"I'll show you who's crazy," Dr. Ritter declared. "I'll prove it to you!"

He grabbed me by the back of the neck.

"Hey! Let go!" I shouted.

He didn't say a word. He just shoved me up to the glass cabinet. He shoved my face close to a row of bottles. Bottle after bottle filled with murky brown plankton.

"Take a bottle, Billy," he ordered. "Any bottle."

He pushed me again, until my forehead nearly knocked a bottle over. Then he let go.

"Go ahead," he repeated. "Choose one."

"Why?" I asked. "Why do you want me to take a bottle?"

"I'll tell you why," Dr. Ritter said. "Because you're going to drink it, Billy. All of it."

30

I stared at the bottles.

"Take one, Billy," Dr. Ritter insisted. "Or I'll take one and pour it down your throat."

I had no choice.

I reached up and picked the last one from the middle shelf.

I stared at it. Disgusting brown and green glop.

Not exactly the breakfast I had in mind.

"Wait till you see this, Dr. Deep," Dr. Ritter said. He stared at me. His eyes gleaming.

"The growth hormone reacted strangely with the plankton," Dr. Ritter explained. "As soon as the boy drinks it, he'll turn into a fish. It takes only a minute or two."

He grabbed the bottle from me. He opened it and handed it back.

"Drink."

I lifted the bottle to my lips.

"No!" Sheena cried.

Dr. D. covered the lip of the bottle with one hand.

"Wait, Billy," he said. "This is ridiculous, Dr. Ritter. Stop this silliness immediately. And let us go."

"I can't do that. I already explained why," Dr. Ritter answered.

"You need help, Dr. Ritter," Dr. D. said. "You're not thinking clearly. You're a brilliant man. You could be a great scientist."

"I *am* a great scientist," Dr. Ritter insisted. "I'm about to prove that to you right now! Drink, Billy!"

Dr. D.'s hand still covered the bottle.

Thank you, Dr. D., I thought.

"You can't be a great scientist if you hurt people," Dr. D. insisted. "Let us go. We'll get you the help you need. Then you can change the world for the better."

"You're an idiot, Dr. Deep," Dr. Ritter sneered. "You'll be the next one to turn into a fish. Just as soon as I finish with the boy."

He swatted Dr. D.'s hand away from the bottle. "Drink that plankton *now*, Billy," he commanded. "Or I'll throw you all overboard."

I swished the brown liquid in the bottle.

I gulped.

It looked so gross.

But what was my choice?

Drown or drink . . .

My hand trembled as I raised the bottle to my lips.

And I drank it down.

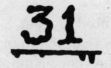

31

I made a disgusted face. My whole body shook.

Then I stood there stiffly. Every muscle tensed. Waiting.

The others stared at me. They didn't move, either.

Sheena's chin trembled. "I don't want you to turn into a fish, Billy! Why did you drink it? Why didn't you throw it on the floor?"

"He would just pick out another bottle for me," I replied hoarsely. I could still taste the liquid in my mouth. I felt it gurgling around in my stomach.

At least a minute passed. Then another minute.

"Okay," Dr. Ritter said. "It should happen — *now!*"

He pointed at me. I stood there. I was still a boy.

"I don't see any changes," Dr. D. said.

"Give it another minute," Dr. Ritter insisted. "I know it works. I tried it on my assistant, Mel, last night. He's swimming around out there playing tag with a blue marlin right now!"

The room fell silent as we all waited for me to turn into a fish.

My stomach felt a little queasy. Otherwise, nothing.

I sighed and shifted my feet.

"It's been more than five minutes, Ritter," Dr. D. said. "Looks like your plankton doesn't work."

Dr. Ritter scowled furiously. "No! That's impossible! It works! I know it works!"

He grabbed me and shook me. "Fish! Turn into a fish!"

I bumped him away. He toppled backwards.

Dr. D. pounced on him. "Gotcha!"

Dr. Ritter pushed him off. And grabbed a bottle of plankton.

He raised the bottle over his head.

"Look out, Dr. D.!" Sheena cried.

Dr. Ritter swung the bottle.

Dr. D. ducked.

I snatched the bottle from Dr. Ritter's hand.

My uncle leaped at Dr. Ritter. Dr. Ritter dodged him and dashed out of the lab.

"He's going up on deck!" Sheena shouted.

We raced after him. Dr. D. tackled Dr. Ritter on the deck. Dr. Ritter rolled away. He jumped on Dr. D.

They wrestled around. I set the bottle of plankton down.

"Get off him!" I yelled. I tried to pull Dr. Ritter off my uncle.

Dr. Ritter elbowed me away. Dr. D. grabbed him. They rolled across the deck.

"Dr. D. — look out!" I screamed. He was about to roll overboard.

With a grunt, Dr. D. jumped to his feet. He dove on Dr. Ritter and pinned him to the deck.

"Get a rope, Billy! Quick!" he ordered.

I grabbed the first rope I found on the deck. "Tie him up!" Dr. D. ordered. "Sheena — help me hold him down."

Sheena took a running start and leaped on top of Dr. Ritter.

Dr. Ritter grunted. "My stomach!"

Sheena sat on top of him. Dr. D. pinned his arms down. I wrapped the rope around his wrists.

Dr. D. had taught me some sailor's knots the summer before. My mind raced, trying to remember them.

How did it go? I thought in a panic. Over, under, around?

Dr. Ritter squirmed under Sheena. "Hurry, Billy!" she snapped.

"I'm trying!" I said.

"It's over, Ritter," Dr. D. said. "We're taking you to the International Sea Life Patrol."

Over, under, over?

"No, you're not!" Dr. Ritter cried. He bucked Sheena off.

She tumbled to the deck.

He wrenched his hands from the rope and shoved Dr. D. away.

My crummy knots were useless.

Dr. D. tried to grab him. But Dr. Ritter dove away and crawled across the deck. He snatched up a bottle of plankton.

He stood and waved the bottle at us. "You'll never turn me in!" he declared.

Then he pulled the bottle open, tilted it over his mouth, and drank it down.

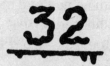

32

"It works!" Dr. Ritter declared. "I'll prove it to you!"

He tossed the bottle aside. The glass smashed on the deck.

"You can't fool us, Dr. Ritter," Sheena said. "We know that stuff doesn't work. We saw Billy drink it."

But Dr. Ritter's body began to tremble. Quickly, his skin began to darken to a slivery, blue-gray.

"Something's happening!" Dr. D. exclaimed.

Dr. Ritter's skin began to flake. Then it turned scaly. It glittered in the sunlight.

His body began to shrink. His clothes slid off the slick scales. His hair fell away. His head flattened. His whole body shrank and flattened.

"It's working!" I gasped. "He's turning into a fish!"

Dr. Ritter's arms shriveled into fins. His legs melted together, melted into a fish tail.

He flopped on the deck. One flat eye stared glassily up at us as he flapped his tail.

"He's a fish!" Sheena cried. "I don't believe it!"

With one great flip of his tail, the fish plopped over the side of the deck and into the water.

We watched him as he dove under the surface.

"Stop him!" I shouted. "He's getting away! We can't let him escape!" I started for my snorkeling flippers.

But Dr. D. squeezed my shoulder. "No, Billy. It's okay. Let him go."

"Huh? Why?"

"You heard what he told us, Billy. Dr. Ritter will be a fish forever," Dr. D. explained. "He can't do anyone any harm now."

I stared down at the silvery fish. It splashed its tail in the water and swam out to sea.

"Wow," Sheena gasped, pressing her hands against her cheeks.

Dr. D. put his arms around us. "I guess that adventure is over," he sighed. "I was never so scared in my life."

Sheena and I agreed. "I'm scared — and amazed," I told my uncle. "I'll never forget the strange things we saw this week."

We followed Dr. D. down to help him prepare breakfast. He stopped in his lab.

· "What a mess," he sighed. "I guess I'll clean it up later."

Sheena walked over to the cabinet of plankton bottles. She turned to me and narrowed her eyes at me. "Hey, Billy — you drank a bottle of plankton too."

I shrugged. "Yeah. So?"

"So why didn't you turn into a fish like Dr. Ritter did?" she demanded.

"You know why," I teased.

"I do not."

"Yes, you do. It's because I'm not human. I'm *super*human."

She punched me in the stomach. "Come on. Tell me the real reason."

Dr. D. folded his arms across his chest. "Yes, Billy. Tell us. I'd be interested to hear this."

I grinned. "Well, it's all thanks to you, Sheena."

"Me?"

"Uh-huh. I was really angry after you played that trick on me. You know, the doll's head in the goldfish bowl?"

Sheena giggled.

"Ha-ha. Hilarious. Anyway, I spent all day and all night trying to think up a good trick to play on you. To get you back."

"That's all you ever do, Billy," Sheena said. "What's so different about that?"

I tapped the cabinet. "I had a great idea. I took one of the plankton bottles and dumped the plankton out."

Dr. D. grimaced. "You what?"

"Sorry, Dr. D.," I said. "I figured you had so many, you wouldn't miss one."

"I still don't get it," Sheena said. "Then what?"

"I washed out the bottle. Then I poured iced tea into it," I explained. "I was going to bring you in here and say, 'Hey, Sheena! Want to see me drink plankton?' Then I'd gulp down the iced tea and totally gross you out!"

"That wouldn't have grossed me out," Sheena protested.

"Yes, it would!" I insisted. "You would've puked all over the cabin floor!"

"No, I wouldn't!"

Dr. D. interrupted us. "You planted a bottle of iced tea in the plankton cabinet? So when Dr. Ritter told you to choose a bottle . . . "

"Right!" I cried. "I picked the bottle of iced tea!"

Sheena laughed. She laughed so hard, she almost choked.

"I know it's funny," I said. "But even *I* don't think it's *that* funny."

She hiccupped and caught her breath. "I don't believe it," she gasped. "You and I are starting to think alike, Billy."

"What do you mean?"

"I played the same trick on you!" she cried. "The exact same trick! I put iced tea in a bottle too. Watch!"

She pulled a bottle from an end of the cabinet, ripped off the stopper, and gulped it down.

Dr. D. and I gaped at her in shock.

Sheena made a weird face. Her eyes bulged. She grabbed her stomach.

"Oh, wow," she groaned. "Did I drink the right bottle?"

Add *more*

Goosebumps®

to your collection . . .

Here's a chilling preview of

RETURN OF THE MUMMY

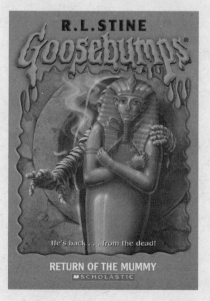

6

The tent was already hot when I awoke the next morning. Bright yellow sunlight poured in through the open tent flap. Squinting against the light, I rubbed my eyes and stretched. Uncle Ben had already gone out.

My back ached. The little cot was so hard!

But I was too excited to worry about my back. I was going down to the pyramid this morning, to the entrance of an ancient tomb.

I pulled on a clean T-shirt and the jeans I'd worn the day before. I adjusted the scarab pendant under the T-shirt. Then I carefully tucked the little mummy hand into the back pocket of my jeans.

With the pendant and the mummy hand, I'm well protected, I told myself. Nothing bad can happen this trip.

I pulled the hairbrush through my thick, black hair a few times, tugged my black-and-yellow

Michigan Wolverines cap on. Then I hurried to the mess tent to get some breakfast.

The sun was floating above the palm trees in the distance. The yellow desert sand gleamed brightly. I took a deep breath of fresh air.

Yuck. There must be some camels nearby, I decided. The air wasn't exactly fresh.

I found Sari and Uncle Ben having their breakfast, seated at the end of the long table in the mess tent. Uncle Ben wore his usual baggy chinos and a short-sleeved, white sportshirt with coffee stains down the front.

Sari had her long, black hair pulled straight back in a ponytail. She wore a bright red tank top over white tennis shorts.

They greeted me as I entered the tent. I poured myself a glass of orange juice and, since I didn't see any Frosted Flakes, filled a bowl with raisin bran.

Three of Uncle Ben's workers were eating at the other end of the table. They were talking excitedly about their work. "We could go in today," I heard one of them say.

"It might take days to break the seal on the tomb door," a young woman replied.

I sat down next to Sari. "Tell me all about the tomb," I said to Uncle Ben. "Whose tomb is it? What's in there?"

He chuckled. "Let me say good morning before I launch into a lecture."

Sari leaned over my cereal bowl. "Hey, look —" she said, pointing. "I got a lot more raisins than you did!"

I *told* you she could turn breakfast into a contest.

"Well, I got more pulp in my orange juice," I replied.

It was just a joke, but she checked her juice glass to make sure.

Uncle Ben wiped his mouth with a paper napkin. He took a long sip of black coffee. "If I'm not mistaken," he began, "the tomb we have discovered here belonged to a prince. Actually, a cousin of King Tutankhamen."

"That's King Tut," Sari told me, interrupting.

"I know that!" I replied sharply.

"King Tut's tomb was discovered in 1922," Uncle Ben continued. "The vast burial chamber was filled with most of Tut's treasures. It was the most amazing archaeological discovery of the century." A smile crossed his face. "Until now."

"Do you think you've found something even more amazing?" I asked. I hadn't touched my cereal. I was too interested in my uncle's story.

He shrugged. "There's no way of knowing what's behind the tomb door until we open it,

Gabe. But I have my fingers crossed. I believe we've found the burial chamber of Prince Khor-Ru. He was the king's cousin. And he was said to be as wealthy as the king."

"And do you think all of Prince Khor-Ru's crowns, and jewels, and belongings are buried with him?" Sari asked.

Uncle Ben took the last sip of coffee and slid the white mug across the table. "Who knows?" he replied. "There could be amazing treasures in there. Or it could be empty. Just an empty room."

"How could it be empty?" I demanded. "Why would there be an empty tomb in the pyramids?"

"Grave robbers," Uncle Ben replied, frowning. "Remember, Prince Khor=Ru was buried sometime around 1300 B.C. Over the centuries, thieves broke into the pyramids and robbed the treasures from many burial chambers."

He stood up and sighed. "We may have been digging for all these months only to find an empty room."

"No way!" I cried excitedly. "I'll bet we find the Prince's mummy in there. And millions of dollars' worth of jewels!"

Uncle Ben smiled at me. "Enough talk," he said. "Finish your breakfast so we can go find out."

Sari and I followed Uncle Ben out of the tent.

He waved to two young men who came out of the supply tent carrying digging equipment. Then he hurried over to talk to them.

Sari and I lingered back. She turned to me, a serious expression on her face. "Hey, Gabe," she said softly, "sorry I've been such a pain."

"You? A pain?" I replied sarcastically.

She didn't laugh. "I'm kind of worried," she confessed. "About Daddy."

I glanced at Uncle Ben. He was slapping one of the young men on the back as he talked. His usual jolly self.

"Why are you worried?" I asked Sari. "Your dad is in a great mood."

"That's why I'm worried," Sari whispered. "He's so happy and excited. He really thinks this is going to be the discovery that makes him famous."

"So?" I demanded.

"So what if it turns out to be an empty room?" Sari replied, her dark eyes watching her father. "What if grave robbers did strip the place? Or what if it isn't that prince's tomb after all? What if Daddy breaks the seal, opens the door — and finds nothing but a dusty, old room filled with snakes?"

She sighed. "Daddy will be heartbroken. Just heartbroken. He's counting on this so much, Gabe.

I don't know if he'll be able to take the disappointment."

"Why look on the gloomy side?" I replied. "What if —"

I stopped because Uncle Ben was hurrying back to us. "Let's go down to the chamber," he said excitedly. "The workers think we are very close to uncovering the tomb entrance."

He put an arm on each of our shoulders and guided us to the pyramid.

As we stepped into the shade of the pyramid, the air grew cooler. The low entrance dug at the bottom of the back wall came into view. It was just big enough for us to enter one at a time. Peering in the narrow hole, I saw that the tunnel dropped steeply.

I hope I don't fall, I thought, a heavy knot of fear tightening my stomach. I pictured myself falling and falling down an endless, dark hole.

Mainly, I didn't want to fall in front of Sari. I knew she'd never let me forget it.

Uncle Ben handed Sari and me bright yellow hard hats. They had lights built into them, like miners' hats. "Stick close together," he instructed. "I remember last summer. You two wandered off and got us into a lot of trouble."

"W-we won't," I stammered. I was trying not to sound nervous, but I couldn't help it.

I glanced at Sari. She was adjusting the yellow hard hat over her hair. She seemed as calm and confident as ever.

"I'll lead the way," Uncle Ben said, pulling the chin strap under his chin. He turned and started to lower himself into the hole.

But a shrill cry from behind us made us all stop and turn around.

"Stop! Please — stop! Don't go in!"

7

A young woman came running across the sand. Her long, black hair flew behind her head as she ran. She carried a brown briefcase in one hand. A camera, strapped around her neck, bobbed in front of her.

She stopped in front of us and smiled at Uncle Ben. "Dr. Hassad?" she asked breathlessly.

My uncle nodded. "Yes?" He waited for her to catch her breath.

Wow. She's really pretty, I thought. She had long, black hair, sleek and shiny. She had bangs cut straight across her forehead. Beneath the bangs were the most beautiful green eyes I'd ever seen.

She was dressed all in white. A white suit jacket and a white blouse over white slacks. She was short — only an inch or two taller than Sari.

She must be a movie star or something, I told myself. She's so great-looking!

She set her briefcase down on the sand and brushed back her long, black hair. "I'm sorry I shouted like that, Dr. Hassad," she told my uncle. "It's just that I needed to talk to you. I didn't want you to disappear into the pyramid."

Uncle Ben narrowed his eyes at her, studying her. "How did you get past the security guard?" he asked, pulling off the hard hat.

"I showed them my press card," she replied. "I'm a reporter for the Cairo *Sun*. My name is Nila Rahmad. I was hoping —"

"Nila?" Uncle Ben interrupted. "What a pretty name."

She smiled. "Yes. My mother named me after the River of Life, the Nile."

"Well, it's a very pretty name," Uncle Ben replied. His eyes twinkled. "But I'm not ready to have any reporters write about our work here."

Nila frowned and bit her lower lip. "I spoke to Dr. Fielding a few days ago," she said.

My uncle's eyes widened in surprise. "You did?"

"Dr. Fielding gave me permission to write about your discovery," Nila insisted, her green eyes locked on my uncle.

"Well, we haven't discovered anything yet!" Uncle Ben said sharply. "There may not be anything to discover."

"That's not what Dr. Fielding told me," Nila replied. "He seemed confident that you were about to make a discovery that would shock the world."

Uncle Ben laughed. "Sometimes my partner gets excited and talks too much," he told Nila.

Nila's eyes pleaded with my uncle. "May I come into the pyramid with you?" She glanced at Sari and me. "I see you have other visitors."

"My daughter, Sari, and my nephew, Gabe," Uncle Ben replied.

"Well, could I come down with them?" Nila pleaded. "I promise I won't write a word for my paper until you give me permission."

Uncle Ben rubbed his chin thoughtfully. He swung the hard hat back onto his head. "No photographs, either," he muttered.

"Does that mean I can come?" Nila asked excitedly.

Uncle Ben nodded. "As an observer." He was trying to act real tough. But I could see he liked her.

Nila flashed him a warm smile. "Thank you, Dr. Hassad."

He reached into the storage cart and handed her a yellow hard hat. "We won't be making any amazing discoveries today," he warned her. "But we're getting very close — to something."

As she slipped on the heavy helmet, Nila turned to Sari and me. "Is this your first time in the pyramid?" she asked.

"No way. I've already been down three times," Sari boasted. "It's really awesome."

"I just arrived yesterday," I said. "So it's my first time down in —"

I stopped when I saw Nila's expression change. Why was she staring at me like that?

I glanced down and realized that she was staring at the amber pendant. Her mouth was open in shock.

"No! I don't believe this! I really don't! This is so *weird*!" she exclaimed.

"Wh-what's wrong?" I stammered.

"We're *twins*!" Nila declared. She reached under her suit jacket and pulled out a pendant she wore around her neck.

An amber pendant, shaped exactly like mine.

"How unusual!" Uncle Ben exclaimed.

Nila grasped my pendant between her fingers and lowered her face to examine it. "You have a scarab inside yours," she told me, turning the pendant around in her fingers.

She dropped mine and held hers up for me to see. "Look, Gabe. Mine is empty."

I gazed into her pendant. It looked like clear orange glass. Nothing inside.

"I think *yours* is prettier," Sari told Nila. "I wouldn't want to wear a dead bug around my neck."

"But it's supposed to be good luck or something," Nila replied. She tucked the pendant back under her white jacket. "I hope it isn't *bad* luck to have an empty one!"

"I hope so too," Uncle Ben commented dryly. He turned and led us into the pyramid opening.

I'm not really sure how I got lost.

Sari and I were walking together behind Uncle Ben and Nila. We were close behind them. I could hear my uncle explaining about how the tunnel walls were granite and limestone.

Our helmet lights were on. The narrow beams of yellow light darted and crisscrossed over the dusty tunnel floor and walls as we made our way deeper and deeper into the pyramid.

The ceiling hung low, and we all had to stoop as we walked. The tunnel kept curving, and there were several smaller tunnels that branched off. "False starts and dead ends," Uncle Ben called them.

It was hard to see in the flickering light from our helmets. I stumbled once and scraped my elbow against the rough tunnel wall. It was surprisingly cool down here, and I wished I had worn a sweatshirt or something.

Up ahead, Uncle Ben was telling Nila about King Tut and Prince Khor-Ru. It sounded to me as if Uncle Ben was trying to impress her. I wondered if he had a crush on her or something.

"This is so thrilling!" I heard Nila exclaim. "It was so nice of Dr. Fielding and you to let me see it."

"Who is Dr. Fielding?" I whispered to Sari.

"My father's partner," Sari whispered back. "But Daddy doesn't like him. You'll probably meet him. He's always around. I don't like him much, either."

I stopped to examine a strange-looking marking on the tunnel wall. It was shaped like some kind of animal head. "Sari — look!" I whispered. "An ancient drawing."

Sari rolled her eyes. "It's Bart Simpson," she muttered. "One of Daddy's workers must have drawn it there."

"I knew that!" I lied. "I was just testing you."

When was I going to stop making a fool of myself in front of my cousin?

I turned back from the stupid drawing on the wall — and Sari had vanished.

I could see the narrow beam of light from her hard hat up ahead. "Hey — wait up!" I called. But the light disappeared as the tunnel curved away.

And then I stumbled again.

My helmet hit the tunnel wall. And the light went out.

"Hey — Sari? Uncle Ben?" I called to them. I leaned heavily against the wall, afraid to move in the total darkness.

"Hey —! Can anybody hear me?" My voice echoed down the narrow tunnel.

But no one replied.

I pulled off the hard hat and fiddled with the light. I turned it, trying to tighten it. Then I shook the whole hat. But the light wouldn't come back on.

Sighing, I strapped the hat back onto my head.

Now what? I thought, starting to feel a little afraid. My stomach began fluttering. My throat suddenly felt dry.

"Hey — can anybody hear me?" I shouted. "I'm in the dark back here. I can't walk!"

No reply.

Where *were* they? Didn't they notice that I had disappeared?

"Well, I'll just wait right here for them," I murmured to myself.

I leaned my shoulder against the tunnel wall — and fell right through the wall.

No way to catch my balance. Nothing to grab on to.

I was falling, falling down through total darkness.

My hands flailed wildly as I fell.

I reached out frantically for something to grab on to.

It all happened too fast to cry out.

I landed hard on my back. Pain shot out through my arms and legs. The darkness swirled around me.

My breath was knocked right out of me. I saw bright flashes of red, then everything went black again. I struggled to breathe, but couldn't suck in any air.

I had that horrible heavy feeling in my chest, like when a basketball hits you in the stomach.

Finally, I sat up, struggling to see in the total darkness. I heard a soft, shuffling sound. Something scraping over the hard dirt floor.

"Hey — can anyone hear me?" My voice came out a hoarse whisper.

Now my back ached, but I was starting to breathe normally.

"Hey — I'm down here!" I called, a little louder.

No reply.

Didn't they miss me? Weren't they looking for me?

I was leaning back on my hands, starting to feel better. My right hand started to itch.

I reached to scratch it and brushed something away.

And realized my legs were itching, too. And felt something crawling on my left wrist.

I shook my hand hard. "What's going on here?" I whispered to myself.

My entire body tingled. I felt soft pinpricks up my arms and legs.

Shaking both arms, I jumped to my feet. And banged my helmet against a low ledge.

The light flickered on.

I gasped when I saw the crawling creatures in the narrow beam of light.

Spiders. Hundreds of bulby, white spiders, thick on the chamber floor.

They scuttled across the floor, climbing over each other. As I jerked my head up and the light swept up with it, I saw that the stone walls were covered with them, too. The white spiders made the wall appear to move, as if it were alive.

Spiders hung on invisible threads from the chamber ceiling. They seemed to bob and float in midair.

I shook one off the back of my hand.

And with a gasp, realized why my legs itched. Spiders were crawling all over them. Up over my arms. Down my back.

"Help — somebody! Please!" I managed to cry out.

I felt a spider drop on to the top of my head.

I brushed it away with a frantic slap. "Somebody — help me!" I screamed. "Can anyone hear me?"

And then I saw something scarier. Much scarier. A snake slid down from above me, lowering itself rapidly toward my face.

About the Author

R.L. Stine's books are read all over the world. So far, his books have sold more than 300 million copies, making him one of the most popular children's authors in history. Besides Goosebumps, R.L. Stine has written the teen series Fear Street, the funny series Rotten School, as well as the Mostly Ghostly series, The Nightmare Room series, and the two-book thriller *Dangerous Girls*. R.L. Stine lives in New York with his wife, Jane, and Minnie, his King Charles spaniel. You can learn more about him at www.RLStine.com.

THE SCARIEST PLACE ON EARTH!

An All-New, All-Terrifying Series From The Master Of Fright!

Goosebumps HorrorLand

REVENGE OF THE LIVING DUMMY
R.L. STINE
SCHOLASTIC

An All-New, All-Terrifying Series From The Master Of Fright!

Goosebumps HorrorLand

CREEP FROM THE DEEP
R.L. STINE
SCHOLASTIC

An All-New, All-Terrifying Series From The Master Of Fright!

Goosebumps HorrorLand

MONSTER BLOOD FOR BREAKFAST!
R.L. STINE
SCHOLASTIC

An All-New, All-Terrifying Series From The Master Of Fright!

Goosebumps HorrorLand

THE SCREAM OF THE HAUNTED MASK
R.L. STINE
SCHOLASTIC

August 2008!

EnterHorrorLand.com